AuthorTube Presents

Bog Hag
an Anthology

AuthorTube Presents

Bog Hag
an Anthology

Un-Edited by *Nicole Ford Thomas*

Works by
Devon Gambrell
Karla Hailer
C.L. Hart
S.D. Huston
Katy Manz
Jayce Maxwell
J. Noble
Jenna O'Malley
Kay Parquet
Rita Slanina
E.L. Summers
Kyle Thomas
Nicole Ford Thomas
Cass Voit
M.M. Ward
Sam Wicker

Quill Cottage Press

Copyright © 2024 Respective Authors

ISBN: 9798343233308

"These letters stay true to the authors' original texts, privileging their intended voices over stylistic consistency throughout the book."
-Jami Attenburg

CONTENTS

Introduction

INTRODUCTION
NICOLE FORD THOMAS

Whether she's crawling across a sweltering bayou or swimming languidly through a swamp, the bog hag watches and waits. Covered in black scales or perhaps slick, green skin, the witch prowls the wetlands at dusk, waiting for some poor soul to wander too close to her snares.

But is that the whole story for the bog hag? Is she destined to be the dark villain that skulks through bogs looking for her meals? What does the bog hag do when she's not hunting through the marshes?

Sixteen writers from the AuthorTube community on YouTube answered the call to explore and reimagine the nefarious bog hag in their own styles, giving us a look into the remaining shreds of humanity within this malevolent witch. I took care to present the author's words with minimal editing, preserving their unique voices and ensuring there is something for every reader within these pages.

As a gentle warning, the works in this anthology are arranged in order of potentially disturbing content.

Sensitive readers are asked to consider how they feel after reading each piece. If you find yourself uncomfortable at any point, I want to sincerely urge you to stop reading there. As the anthology progresses, the works become more graphic in various ways. Only you can know your threshold, so please practice mindfulness and self-care as you read.

And with that, I am pleased to welcome you to the bog.

-NFT

WHISPERS FROM THE WILLOWS & WEEPING MIRE
S.D. HUSTON

Mist curled around twisted trees of the Weeping Mire, clinging to the thick air as if it were alive. The bog hummed with ancient magic, a low, insistent pulse echoing through murky waters and gnarled roots.

Magic and mist clung to Nimra, tightening around her like chains. It seeped through the cracks in her bog hag's rough skin. Skeletal branches reached for her with greedy fingers, mocking her frailty. The trees had once been her home as a Wood Fae, but now they offered no solace.

He was coming.

Her breath was shallow, and she barely dared to move.

Rion.

The name echoed in the hollow spaces of her stolen body, a bittersweet ache intensifying the real bog hag's own resentment. A venomous whisper against her mind, feeding on her fear. *He's coming to kill you. He has to. You're a monster.*

Her heart pounded as Rion drew closer. The hag had whispered of this day, taunting her, ever since the bog hag had claimed her body, trapping her soul inside while controlling her every movement.

He wouldn't see her—he would see the monster. He would see the creature responsible for the rot in the village's woods, for the blight that had poisoned their home.

Tears pricked at her eyes, hot and stinging against the leathery texture of the bog hag's cheek. He didn't know. He couldn't possibly understand that beneath this grotesque mask, beneath the layers of magic woven into stolen flesh, she was still there.

I'm here! It's me. Nimra.

The girl who laughed beneath the summer sun, the girl who dared him to chase fireflies, the girl who had, foolishly, naively, fallen in love with his easy smile and the warmth in his eyes.

The crunch of leaves underfoot sent a jolt of terror through her. He was close.

And he would kill her.

She drew in a shuddering breath, the air thick with the cloying scent of decay that clung to her like a curse. The bog hag's magic amplified every fear, twisted every thought, and yet, beneath it all, she felt a flicker of desperate hope.

Maybe, just maybe, he would recognize her.

She tried to cry out, but the bog hag's curse tightened around her throat. Her voice, if it escaped, would come out as a rasp, a growl that would only confirm she was a creature to be destroyed. She clenched her fists, struggling to hold on to herself.

He wouldn't know it was her. He couldn't.

Through the swirling mist, pale light filtering through the trees outlined his silhouette. *Rion.* Even now, her heart ached with a familiar pang. She had always loved the way he carried himself, even before everything had fallen apart, back when they were children in the village, back when he was just the boy who used to watch her from across the square.

Her fingers twitched at her side. She tried to call his name, to make him see her, but when she opened her mouth, nothing but a low rasp escaped. The bog hag's curse still too strong. Her mind flashed to a moment from their past—a summer festival in the village where they had first flirted beneath the glowing trees. Her chest tightened at the memory of how close they once were.

Please, let me speak. Let me show him who I am.

He thinks you're the bog hag, the voice whispered, laced with malicious glee. *He sees nothing but the monster.*

He emerged from the swirling mist and stepped into the clearing. His eyes had always held her captive. Now they were narrowed, hardened, reflecting the cold determination of a savior on a mission to slay the creature terrorizing their village.

He stood tall and proud, sunlight glinting off the polished surface of his sword, ready to kill her.

"Show yourself, hag," he growled, his voice like gravel. "I've come to end this."

She took a step back, her pulse racing. Her body moved instinctively, the bog hag's influence still weighing her down. She wanted to scream, to tell him that it was her—that she was still here, still fighting—but no words came, strangled by the magic.

His eyes flicked to her, and for a moment, something flashed across his face. Hesitation? Recognition? She couldn't tell. She reached for that sliver of doubt, clinging to it like a lifeline.

She tried again to speak, her voice a strangled rasp. "Rion, please."

The sound died in the stillness of the bog, swallowed by the ever-present fog. He didn't react, didn't even flinch. He took a step closer, his gaze never leaving hers. His face hardened.

Her heart broke. He didn't see her. He couldn't see her. To him, she was the bog hag, the creature that had cursed their village and taken everything from them.

He doesn't recognize you. He never will.

Her vision blurred. Memories, sharp and painful, flickered through her mind. The summer festival in the village, the scent of woodsmoke and roasted nuts, the feel of his hand brushing against hers as they reached for the same candied apple. Their laughter echoing through the square, his eyes, sparkling with mischief as bright as the paper lanterns strung between the trees.

"Rion please," she whispered, her voice cracking. "Don't remember?"

He shifted, a flicker of uncertainty crossing his face. But it was gone as quickly as it appeared, replaced by a steely resolve. In that moment, all she saw was a stranger, his features hardened with suspicion and disgust.

He lunged.

The sword arced toward her, and she barely managed to dodge, her feet slipping on the damp ground.

She reacted instinctively, the bog hag's magic lending her a speed and agility she hadn't possessed in life. She twisted out of his reach, his blade whistling through the air where she'd been standing a moment before.

But the movement came naturally to her, just like it had in the woods when they used to spar together. Back then, it had been playful—a way to pass the time between chores, a way for them to be close without saying what they both felt.

He stopped, his sword hovering in the air. His eyes narrowed, watching her closely.

"You fight like..." His voice trailed off, confusion flickering in his eyes.

Fight him! The hag's voice urged her on. *Make him suffer like he will make you suffer!*

She stumbled back, a sob catching in her throat. *No.* This wasn't her fight. She wouldn't let the bog hag control her, wouldn't let her poison the memory of what they'd had.

She had to do something. She had to break through the bog hag's curse, had to make him remember.

She opened her mouth to speak, but her voice came out as a rasp again, a growl that sounded nothing like her. The curse tightened around her throat, and panic surged through her chest. *I have to break through. He won't see me if I don't.*

"Remember summer festival? You promised. Take me to next one."

Words tumbled out, desperate and fragmented. But he didn't seem to hear. He pressed his attack, each swing of his sword aimed to kill.

"Stop playing tricks," he said. "I won't fall for your lies."

She dodged and weaved, her movements mirroring the way they used to spar in the forest, their laughter echoing through the trees. Each parry, each near miss, painfully reminded her of what she'd lost, what the bog hag had stolen from her.

He's going to kill you, the voice hissed, cold and sharp. *He sees the monster you've become.*

Despair threatened to consume her. He wasn't even trying to recognize her, to see past the bog hag's grotesque mask, the witch's influence was too strong.

She backed away, her mind racing. Then another memory flashed—their first kiss, beneath the ancient oak tree at the edge of the village. The way he'd cupped her face in his hands, his touch hesitant yet filled with yearning. The air warm with the scent of pine and earth.

She had laughed at something he said, and then... his lips had brushed hers, soft and uncertain.

And his true name, whispered against her lips like a promise. A fae name she alone knew, a bond forged in that stolen moment beneath the whispering leaves when he pledged himself to her.

"Thalrion," she whispered, her voice barely audible over the sound of the wind.

He froze.

"What did you say?"

"Thalrion," she said again, the curse loosening just enough for her to force the word out. "We kissed."

The world seemed to hold its breath. He faltered, his sword arm dropping slightly. His eyes, wide with disbelief, met hers. For a heartbeat, she saw a glimmer of the boy she knew—the one who had been too shy to ask her to dance, the one who had given her flowers and taught her how to spar. The one who had promised to take her to the festival.

He looked at her as if seeing her for the first time, his eyes searching her face for the truth.

"No," he said, but there was doubt in his voice now, doubt that she could see widening the cracks in the bog hag's curse.

But then he shook his head, as if dispelling a dream. "What trickery is this?" he growled, his voice raw. "The bog hag's illusions won't work on me."

"No illusion!" she cried, her voice ragged. "Me! Nimra!"

He advanced again, his movements less certain now, but his purpose unwavering.

She knew she couldn't keep this up forever, tiring, the bog hag's magic a double-edged sword that both protected and consumed her.

She had to make him see. She had to try again to reach him before it was too late.

With trembling fingers, she fumbled with the tangle of vines and leaves cloaking her body, her heart pounding against her ribs. *The wildflower.* The tiny, delicate bloom he'd tucked behind her ear on that magical night beneath the oak tree. She'd pressed it between the pages of her journal, a journal she'd snuck back into the village for when the bog hag had switched their souls.

She found the flower tucked away in the worn leather, its petals brittle with age, but its color still vibrant.

"Gave me this," she said, holding it out to him, an offering, a prayer. "You. Rion. Me."

Time seemed to stop. He stared at the flower, his eyes widening as recognition dawned on his face. He lowered his sword, his entire body seeming to sag with the weight of what he was seeing.

"Nim?" His voice was barely a whisper, choked with disbelief and something akin to hope. "But I just left you in our village."

"Still no believe?" Tears spill down her cheeks.

Through the protest of her aching muscles, the ever-present pull of the bog hag's magic. She placed her hand against the rough bark of a nearby willow, hoping it'd recognized her as a Wood Fae trapped in this body.

The leaves above her shimmered, their edges glowing with a faint, ethereal light in response to her touch. The scent of honeysuckle and pine filled the air, a familiar comfort in the midst of the bog's decay. The magic of the woods—her magic—was still alive, still part of her.

Even dying in this bog, the willow offered its life, its energy, to her. She bowed her head, praying to the Mother goddess, thanking the tree.

Her voice gained strength. "The forest still knows me," she whispered. "And so should you."

He stumbled back, his sword clattering to the ground. He stared at her, his gaze moving from her face to the glowing leaves slowly dying, then back again.

And in his eyes, she saw it. Recognition. Regret.

And something else. Hope.

WORD WITCH? NO, BABBING WORDA
JENNA O'MALLEY

Word Witch? No, Babbing Worda.

Dear child o' mine, do not wonder and

Wander you might to the wood beyond our

Sacred glen. You are not safe beyond that salty

Circle, my child. The Word Witch craves your voice.

Father, loving true, you might have crossed

This kind creature once, but I am your daughter,

Which does not make me you.

Dear child o' mine, you know not which you say

You know this creature as kind and merry, may

You look at the reflection. What you see is not algae

And dead earth so green. Rather slime and grime—

the kind of bones and meat. Of limbs and more left

to rot into her flesh. In this case, the words she steals are

not from your throat but from your chest.

They are your life. Your dreams. You could never return if

You venture beyond the circle and deep into the trees.

Father, the wisps call me to dance, and the trees are my protection

As I hop from branch to branch. Dance I do, and dance I dare.

You could fall and trip into her snare.

Dear child o' mine, where are you walking?

Are you watching what you say?

Father, she listens.

She calls.

To her I must return.

She is my mother.

And it is with her my magic grows

And it is with her I shall learn.

Dear child o' mine, run back home.

Home?

Father, your poison shoved who I was in my heart,

In my home, into the unknown.

I belong to the wind,

To the wastes.

To the flames.

To the decaying rebirth that creeps along in nature's veins.

I am my home, for with you I cannot be

In a world where magic does not exist

Where a girl becomes a woman who is not allowed to dance and talk to the trees.

How To Be the Best Bog Hag You Can Be In Ten Easy Steps
J. Noble

Good morning my fellow witches! Today we are going to spend some time discussing our fellow Bog Hags.

BOG HAG:

(Unfair definition)

Vile, swamp-dwelling hags, heinous crones that prey on humans.

#

DISCLAIMER:

Bog Hag is no longer strictly a female dominated life. As with all witches, we welcome everyone. Be you male, female, Fae, and everything in-between. We are all inclusive.

#

Cranky and Semi-Approachable

-Semi-approachable is key. You want the desperate and needy coming to you. You don't want them to stay but you do want their business.

-Frowning and short curt answers are a must. Except toward children. Children are innocent and loved.

#

Home Environment

-On the outside, your home should blend in with its surroundings. Vines, moss, many types of plants that are used in various spells and potions are always the best to use at decoration.

-Inside, be inventive. Be you. The main room, where you will be receiving your 'customers', should be dim and foreboding. Beyond that, create a home you love. Bright and cheery, mellow and spiritual. There is

no limit. Be sure no one goes beyond the main room if you want to

maintain your Bog Hag Status.

#

Your Familiar

-Cats, Crows, Owls, and Toads are your expected familiars. If

that's what works for you then by all means, have one of those.

-Unique familiars, can be a blast, just for the shock and awe

factor.

-Such as:

-Snakes, possums, skunks, etc. The stranger the

better.

#

Your Crazy Laugh

-You will need to create and nurture a laugh that will attract

attention and repel at the same time. The closer to a cackle the better.

#

Spells, Potions, Talismans/Charms

-Now, this one is important. You want your magic to be powerful enough to work, but not to last forever. You will need them coming back for more. You are trying to make a living without looking like you are trying.

-Make sure you label all of your vials and jars clearly. Dates and what they are used for. This way it will be easier for you choose the best one for whatever issue is needed.

#

Payment for Services

-Money is nice, but most of your 'customers' are too poor to pay in cash. Getting inventive with payment can be fun and very lucrative at times.

-First born children, animals, and souls are always a welcome bargaining tool for your services. Secrets, especially deep dark secrets, are the best. You can use them to gain the upper hand when it's needed to make sure you are left alone to run your business and enjoy your life.

#

Cauldron

-This one is a given. Always keep a cauldron bubbling in your front yard or main room. The bigger the better. It makes the 'customers' nervous not knowing what your brewing up. Is it laundry? Soup? Bones of your enemies? Who knows?

#

Speak in Riddles and Confusing Premonitions

-Be sure to be vague and confusing when giving advice. This way no matter how things turn out you can't be blamed.

-as for premonitions, always make sure that there are more than one way for things to turn out. This way, as with advice, you cannot be blamed for anything going sideways. Because, let's face it, people are stupid and will misinterpret anything and everything you say, no matter how good your intentions are.

#

Keep Your Hexing to a Minimum

-One or two a year is best. But make sure they aren't too extreme. We don't need a mob showing up on your doorstep in the middle of the night.

-Also, make sure they can be blamed on natural occurrences or accidents to detour the true blame from you.

#

There you are witches. These are only ten ways to be the best Bog Hag you can be. There are many other ways that can be learned but we will touch on those another time. Be safe my friends. Be free and be you.

#

This post is brought to you by:

Tipsy's Jar Emporium

We've got jars for all your witchy needs.

25% off your entire purchase if you bring your familiar in to meet us!

Open Monday-Friday Dawn to dusk.

ALLURING ENCHANTRESS
E.L. SUMMER

Alluring Enchantress

In the heart of the swamp,
where the fog clings tight
and mist envelopes all,

A slumbering demon roams
enveloping a monstrous woman
cloaked in desolation,

From her aura
frost seeps into the night,
eyes flickering like dying coals
in the dead of night.

Children's merriment
drift through the trees,
nightingales melody drawing them near

Masquerading as a guided voice
luring them deeper into her domain
hoping to feed her belly
and satisfy the spirits of the nevermore

The swamp murmurs her name,
caution to those
who dare approach,

For the swamp witch lies in wait,
ravenous and sly,
in the void of night,
where fears come alive.

A Bog Hag Slaps a Fish
Rita Slanina

"'Slap a fish, win a witch,' my ma used to always say."

"Huh?" Clarice stared at the man, who stood behind the seafood counter in the bustling marketplace.

"You've never heard that saying before?" He grinned, revealing a set of crooked teeth.

Clarice had always had interesting interactions with folks in this peculiar town, but this one was a doozy.

Clarice grew up in a small town whose best attributes were boasted by the sign at the edge of town:

A little witchy like Salem, A lot swampy like Sleepy Hollow.

Population: 666.

Yeah. Inviting, isn't it?

Clarice had always thought that one day she'd leave this place, one day. But naturally, that day never came, and here she was watching a man fish out her dinner from a bucket. Travelers, from near and far, would visit, passing through the town faster than a witch's broom could take them.

Every night, something eerie would encroach upon the town, something with a deep hunger for flesh and bones. And, in part, Clarice was responsible. A mild shiver ran down her spine at the thought.

"Here ya go, one fish 'wich!" The man tossed her wrapped meal on the counter next to the cash register, startling her out of her thoughts.

"I'm not a witch," Clarice stated with a scowl, feeling her temper rise.

The man started laughing, shaking his head, as he grabbed her fish 'wich to ring up her order.

Walking back to her home, the trees around her bent towards her as she passed, sprinkling the falling leaves of autumn's descent into darkness. The winding road ahead of her appeared to dance as her feet stepped on the hot tar of the curvy road.

Clarice waved a finger and slid her crossbody bag behind her, readying to fly the rest of the way home. Out of thin air, a broom grew from a pencil discreetly hidden inside her bag to a useful device for travel. Filling the space beneath her, she casually sat upon the now visible broom, picking her up to glide home.

Hopping off her ride, her feet firmly touched the ground, and the broom set itself aside at the front door. Clarice's front porch, which looked like a typical neighborhood home from the 1950s, slowly deformed into its true sinister appearance.

Anyone who passed by only saw what she wanted them to see. There were no visible cobwebs, potions, or cauldrons for passersby, but they were there.

You see, Clarice was a witch. But she never asked to be one. She wanted to grow up and get the heck outta this small town. But people from Caillech Willowstown never left. The townspeople were trapped there by a curse.

You wouldn't think of Caillech Willowstown as a cursed and trapped area. It was beautifully manicured to the likeness of a quaint country town in one of your favorite romance movies. Maybe if you saw the tourists passing through, you'd understand. The snarky store owners who meandered into the off-the-beaten-path village, who decided to make this place their home, were none the wiser. Oh, they'd heard the rumors, but the witches had done their best to maintain anonymity. They had done so to protect themselves.

When these newbies came into town and realized there were real live witches and warlocks, there was an uptick in abusing them, torturing them, forcing them into cages to manifest special favors, and casting spells to get gold, treasures, money, and even love potions.

Knock. Knock. Knock.

Clarice was startled out of her daydreaming about the day she'd escape this proverbial glass prison. Who could that be? She knew that whenever she reached the edge of town, she'd be thrown right back inside her cottage. No spells, tails, or magic dust was getting her out of here. She'd tried.

Opening the door, she rubbed her eyes, "Hello?"

"Hi!" A youthful, cheerful man with tousled hair and a smile that could melt hearts waved. "I'm Beau, and I'm looking for work. Do you need anything fixed around here?"

Before Clarice could respond, a loud crash came from behind her house. The sound of splintering wood and breaking glass echoed through the silent evening.

"What was that?" Beau asked, his eyes wide with surprise.

Clarice's heart pounded as she rushed to the back of the house, with Beau close on her heels. There, in the clearing behind her home, stood a grotesque creature—a monstrous, skeletal figure shrouded in tatters, with glowing green eyes burning with malice.

"It's come for me!" Clarice whispered, dread filling her heart.

"For you? What is that thing?" Beau asked, horrified, and then added, "Wait a minute, what did you mean it's come for you?"

"The Bone Reaper," Clarice explained hurriedly. "It hunts witches, seeking to claim their souls for eternal torment. I've been hiding from it for years, and tonight is the last night of its haunting season. If we survive till dawn, it will be banished for another year."

Beau looked bewildered. "You're a witch?" The realization dawned on him just as the creature let out a bone-chilling howl. "And you didn't think to mention this before?"

Clarice grabbed her broom from the porch, muttering an incantation under her breath. The ground beneath them trembled, and a protective barrier started to form, glowing faintly.

"I didn't think it was relevant! Now focus! Keep it busy while I strengthen the spell!" Clarice instructed. "And don't get caught!"

Beau looked around, found a garden rake, and waved it in front of the fearsome creature. "Hey! Over here, big guy!" The Bone Reaper turned its ghastly gaze toward Beau and charged.

Beau watched in tense silence as Clarice stepped forward, her eyes narrowing with determination. She took a deep breath, and with a whisper of ancient incantations, she began to transform.

Her delicate features twisted and contorted; her hair turned into wild, snake-like tendrils, and her skin adopted a sickly green hue spotted with warts. Her nose grew long and crooked, and her fingernails extended into sharp, claw-like talons. Clarice's true form as a bog hag was horrifyingly grotesque, and as the transformation completed, she now exuded a terrifying magical aura.

Beau's jaw dropped. "Whoa! Clarice, you look like my Aunt Gertrude on a bad hair day! No wonder you keep this under wraps!" he blurted out, struggling to contain his laughter amidst the razor-edge tension.

Clarice threw him a sideways glance, something between a smirk and a snarl. "Focus, Beau! I need your help to distract the Bone Reaper while I tap into my full power."

Without missing a beat, Beau grabbed a nearby frying pan and started banging it like a makeshift drum. "Hey Bonehead! Over here! You can't handle the sizzle of this sorceress stew!"

Clarice rolled her eyes but couldn't help a chuckle. Beau's antics were absurd, yet endearing, and they provided just the boost of confidence she needed. As the Bone Reaper turned its gaze towards Beau's cacophony, she harnessed her unrestrained swamp hag magic and unleashed a torrent of enchanted energy.

Exhausted, Clarice and Beau collapsed onto the ground, breathing heavily.

"Thanks for helping," Clarice said, looking at Beau appreciatively.

"No problem," Beau replied, chuckling. "You know, this is not exactly what I had in mind when I said I needed work."

Clarice laughed for the first time in what felt like ages. "Welcome to Caillech Willowstown."

Beau, glanced around nervously, and said, "So, does this job come with hazard pay?"

Clarice snorted, unable to contain her laughter. "Oh, absolutely. How do you feel about being paid in fish 'wiches?"

Beau looked mock-serious. "As long as I don't have to actually slap any more fish."

With the sun rising and the Bone Reaper banished, the two new allies found themselves laughing and planning their next move, starting with a well-deserved breakfast.

SLUDGE AND SPARKLES
M.M. WARD

Chapter One

The enchanted cottage settled in the vacant lot. Overgrown weeds and random trash suited its dilapidated appearance of weathered planks and dirty windows. Its chicken legs folded out of sight as it nested on the unkempt land. Glamoured to look like a maiden in a boho-styled sundress, Ewenoe Yaga walked around it to make certain her home's special traits were hidden by the knee-high grass and weeds. The sun was sinking toward the horizon. It had been a long day and night of travel for them.

"Are you comfortable?" She asked the building, and it shuddered in the affirmative. "Thank you for bringing me, House."

Going inside, Ewenoe tied her bag to her waist and wrapped her shawl over her shoulder haunch. Fluffing her hair to cover the hump before she closed the door, she glanced at the piece of parchment then she started toward the address. Knowing the invitation and map would be burned once she arrived, she dropped an enchanted pebble every tenth step. The tiny gray rocks would glow purple in a way only she would be able to see. Her great-aunt Gretel taught her the value of not relying on memory to find her way home. Long ago, Gretel and her brother Hansel were lost in the primeval forest of the old country and were taken in by her great-grandmother's sister. Mad bog hag Orba Yaga tried to eat the children. Breaking the first law of the Yagas, harm no child and rescue those endangered. Gretel killed Orba by pushing her into an oven and gained her power thus becoming a Yaga bog hag herself. Baba adopted Gretal as a daughter. The history of mythology had been twisted to make the bog hags seem like a threat to all because of their murderous inclination to eat humans and monsters who were criminals or harmed children.

That was in the old country centuries ago, but now in the modern world, vast human cities where the new wilderness and supernaturals were only welcomed if they looked a certain way or acted as shills of the ruling authorities, the Supernatural Supervision Society. Only the oldest families and clans knew the S.S.S. was controlled by a human council who were secretly corrupt mages and the demon-possessed. The bridge-dweller and cave-dweller clans of orcs, ogres, and trolls were the first to sign up to work for the S.S.S., despite their appearance and criminal tendencies.

She hated those traitors in the supernatural world who became the paper-pushing bureaucrats and enforcers of the Supernatural Supervision Society, because they used their authority to bully and cause harm. Ewenoe ground her teeth, wishing they still lived under bridges or caves and acted as criminals so she could legally eat them. It gave her glamour of being a brunette maiden with an eclectic style, an angry and horrific expression while the pebbles fell one at a time from her fingers in measured increments.

Thinking about what she was after tonight, her unnatural grin widened until it stretched almost to her ears showing her pointed teeth.

A young man who started to approach her veered away and ran across the street. She tracked him with a bird-like movement. The jerk of her head pulled her hair enough to uncover her haunch.

"She's a ghoul!" The wide-eyed, young human shouted at his two friends who were trying to sneak up behind her.

When she looked over her shoulder, flashing them a shark's smile, they froze then sprinted away. She knew what they wanted, to rob and accost her glamour. She could smell their evil intent in their scents. She shook her head, resettling her hair. They smelled good, young and meaty with cannabis and alcohol infused into their soft flesh. The criminals would have been delicious with a citrus marinade and cabbage slaw.

Dropping a pair of pebbles at the corner before glancing again at the parchment map, she turned down another street which went between two warehouses. Four pebbles were left behind with their ten steps between, and then she turned again, dropping three pebbles this time. She left no more markers on the sidewalk of the last street, lest the doorman see her marking her path. As she approached the door, her feet cramped in the weathered boots that looked too big for her size. She resisted the urge to kick them off and stretch her clawed toes. Following the wall of the warehouse, she glanced up to where it loomed large and windowless above her. A single green door with a troll leaning next to a fire barrel waited. Ewenoe realized she was dressed inappropriately for the temperature of the human city, but it didn't matter, she had reached her destination.

"The S.S.S. were fools to let trolls join their ranks. They are nothing but corrupt hoarders whose only loyalty is to the gold in their pocket," she thought in disdain.

Ewenoe held out the map and three gold coins, "I'm here for the meeting?"

The troll tossed her parchment invitation into the fire; it burned with the color of vermilion and ochre. The three coins went into a hidden pocket in his vest. "Welcome." He said in a neutral voice, but he shuddered as he looked her up and down seeing what she truly was with the shimmer of discernment magic on his glasses.

Ewenoe grinned wickedly, showing all her hideous glory because he could see her as she truly was. "Thank you. Are there any orcs in the pool tonight?"

"Orcs? Maybe one or two who didn't win the mating lottery... Why would a bog hag want to date an orc?" The troll eyed her suspiciously.

"I like my males large and my sausages thick. The swamp which I talked to last time said orcs are the biggest and thickest, not stringy or tiny like trolls who have no meat on their bones." Looking down on the creature half her height, she leaned forward and snapped her pointed teeth at him.

"Eh...Uhm, eating other s-s-s-supernaturals or humans is f-f-forbidden," the troll stammered.

Cackling laughter burst from Ewenoe's lips then she lied, "Oh tiny troll, who said anything about dinner? I'm just here for the after-party sex."

A velvety smooth chuckle rolled over her with seductive vibrations. "With a glamour like that, I'm certain you'll find it." The scent of fresh blood, wine, and tomb dust followed the words to Ewenoe's sensitive nose.

The troll's eyes widened as he stared past Ewenoe. She turned to see who had sneaked up on her. A vampire stood sparkling in the twilight. He held out a parchment invitation map to the troll and one gold coin.

"I'm here for the meeting."

Ewenoe seized the troll's wrist when he took the coin. "Why does he only have to pay one when I paid three? Are you trying to cheat me, bridge-dweller?"

Trembling in fear as he stared at her teeth, the troll tried to wretch his arm free. "Males are harder to get to come to these events... We have expenses to cover."

The vampire pulled her hand from the troll's wrist gently. Sparkles glittering on her skin where he touched her. "Come with me, my lady witch, and I'll buy your first drink to make up for it?" He grinned at the troll showing fangs as long as the troll's pinky finger, "Open the door now."

There was power behind those words Ewenoe didn't miss, and something tweaked a memory she inherited from her great-grandmother Baba. Before she had time to pursue it, the vampire guided her inside with a hand at the small of her back.

Inside the rundown-looking warehouse, there was a lobby and then a ballroom filled with small tables, side by side, and two chairs at each table. A carved wooden bar ran along one wall. It looked like the inside of a five-star hotel she saw in a brochure once. There were groups of supernaturals mingling and talking. Many were wearing white name tags and holding elaborate drinks. She nodded her head at the few witches of different species that she knew. Several were openly staring at her unexpected companion. Her nose twitched, taking in the scents.

'Yes, there are orcs and ogres here... and werewolves, werebears, and a fae. Interesting,' she pondered the reason, and the only one that made sense worried her.

Chapter Two

"Well, let's get you a drink. I'm Devlin," he murmured as she noticed he sniffed her hair.

As she stepped away, she tipped her head at him, "You know what I am under this glamour, don't you?"

"I don't mind if you don't mind what I am without a glamour." He smiled handsomely and sparkled a little more. "Your name?" He waved at the Fae who was tending bar.

"Ewenoe" She answered, "And I don't mind either."

His handsome features scrunched up as the Fae stepped toward them, "No, I don't know... Bordeaux blood wine, O-negative, if you have it and whatever the witch wants." He sounded confused and she laughed looking at his expression.

She noted the bartender's covetous scent and jealous demeanor as she glanced at the handsome vampire. Ewenoe glanced at the fae's un-cleavage, then smirked, crossing her arms under her excessive chest and drew an envious glance. "They're real, not a glamour if you're wondering... And I'll have what he's having."

They stood in silence as the drinks were made, before taking the glasses. The fae took the gold coin Devlin offered but didn't give him any change.

"Don't forget to register," the fae grumbled then went to serve two elemental fire witches who were laughing as they snuffed and relit the candelabra at the end of the bar.

"I still don't know your name," Devlin scowled, as they walked away toward the registration table.

The expression would be handsome to a human, witch, or monster who didn't know what vampires were meant to be. Suddenly everything beautiful about him seemed so wrong as she remembered where her great-grandmother smelled his flesh scent before.

She decided she needed to formally greet him. "I am Ewe-noe Yaga, Lord Devlin Drakul," Ewenoe slowly pronounced her first name then said his full name and title with the accent and language of the old country.

Admiration shined in his eyes. "I am honored to meet you."

She went to sip her wine and paused. It smelled faintly of witch's bane to her sensitive nose, and she knew it contained a de-scented tincture of the toxic plant. She put her hand on his arm, stopping him from drinking.

"May I hold your wine while you register us, Duncan?" She suggested quickly, then sniffed his glass too.

He looked at her oddly because she purposely mispronounced his name, but then the troll at the table pushed name tag stickers and marker at him with two numbered plastic coins.

"Write your name and your species. No clamors once the rounds begin. This is just a meet and greet and not speed dating. Dating or seeking a mate outside the supernatural lottery is illegal. Do you understand?" The troll working the table demanded.

"Yes," they both responded as the troll turned the registration book.

Devlin wrote 'Duncan Rose' in elegant calligraphy on the name tag, then he wrote the word 'Vampire' beneath the name.

"Spell your name for me, lovely."

Ewenoe hesitated, then gave the name of a mermaid she ate with a friend for seducing and killing teenaged human males. "Audora Waters. A-U-D-O-R-A."

He wrote it and smiled at the troll as he wrote the word 'Witch' underneath.

"You have to write that she's a sea witch," the troll demanded in a waspish tone, so Devlin added the word to her name tag.

Ewenoe didn't correct him that she was a bog hag and not a sea

35

witch. What the trolls didn't know, they didn't know, and this young one obviously had never met enough kinds of witches to know there were differences. He started signing the registration book with their fake names and species when the troll interrupted him. "She has to sign for herself."

Ewenoe scrawled her alias unintelligibly then the vampire signed with a flourish, leaving a residue of sparkles behind where his hand brushed the page. While the troll was distracted studying what Devlin wrote and trying to dust off the sparkles, Ewenoe reached into her bag and palmed two cat's claw roots. She stuck her name tag on her shawl while he put his on the trendy scarf around his neck. As they walked away, he took his glass but didn't drink.

"You can smell it too?" She whispered the question as more creatures moved from the bar to the registration table.

"Why would they dose the drinks to prevent the use of magic?" Devlin murmured over the lip of his glass, pretending to take a sip.

"Maybe because drunk witches and monsters are dangerous?" Ewenoe said before she pressed one of the roots into his palm under the pretense of squeezing his hand. "Keep this under your tongue and it will counteract the bane if you have to take a sip. Thank you for trying to buy me a drink." She started to walk away toward a group of witches she knew then paused to look at him. "I'm really sorry your kind was cursed to be... This pretty." She waved her hand to indicate his appearance.

He looked defeated as he nodded in understanding. "If my uncle hadn't... That witch not only cursed us but wrote those books to make certain the majority collective consciousness believed we looked this way, and now we do. I have spent my whole life looking for a cure, but nothing has worked." He sounded so despairing she pitied him and wondered if somewhere in her family's vast knowledge she could remember a cure.

"I hope you find someone who doesn't mind you're sparkly and pretty," Ewenoe said then she melted out of her glamour to show her true form to him for a moment. The boho-styled sundress and shawl still clung to her curves and covered her haunch, but her skin returned to its grayish appearance. Her features became more birdlike, and her teeth more pointed between her moss-green lips.

As she stood in front of him with skin as mottled as a corpse, but still smooth with youth, he was tempted to touch her cheek. However, that was close to her teeth, and it might cost him a fingertip or his whole hand. Devlin caught his breath then swore quietly, his tone wistful, "Blood of the dead, you're so hideous."

Ewenoe grinned widely showing more of her teeth, "Thank you. I know."

"So why are you looking for an orc?" To stop staring at her, he looked around.

"Orc or ogre, either will do. There's a recipe I need meat and bones for," she murmured quietly as the glamour returned.

"That sounds delicious... I could love a witch who makes food from scratch." He smiled his most charmingly and she wanted to claw his handsomeness off his face because it was so unsuited to him. He didn't deserve to be cursed with beauty, and she was certain he would be absolutely dreadful without his sparkles, raven hair, and male-model features.

"It was nice to meet you, Duncan," she said as the fae bartender walked past carrying a tray.

"And you, Audora."

Slightly saddened, she wandered away to chat with some of the witches she knew. She greeted them and offered a bit of cat's claw root to several. A voodoo witch priestess named Arabella glared around her. She glanced at Ewenoe's name tag and nodded. She had also written a false name above her actual species. Unfortunately, Arabella could not hide what she was as easily as Ewenoe. She was also covertly handing out cat's claw roots to the witches around her.

"I am not liking this, my haggie friend. I not be knowing many of the males here tonight. Why would a werewolf and a minotaur be at a mixer looking for witchy mates?" Arabella murmured as she pretended to sip from a coconut cup.

"Why is there a fae tending bar and handing out tainted drinks?" Ewenoe muttered back to her. "There has never been one here before. I feel like we should leave but I don't know if they would let us go."

"Maybe it's because of all the missing children lately," a demure garden witch whispered. The ivy in her hair was slight yellow matching the scent of her worry.

"What missing children?" Ewenoe demanded but she didn't get an answer.

Chapter Three

There was a gong like the deep tone of a large bell. "Witches and monsters, please find your number and sit down. The rounds will start in a few minutes. The time of each round will be five minutes starting at the tone of the bell, when the bell sounds again the monster males will move to their left. Please remove your glamours now if you have not already done so," the troll from the registration table ordered loudly.

As they separated and moved to find their seats, she noticed Devlin tuck the cat's claw root in his mouth with a fake cough. She hoped he knew not to swallow it. His posture seemed more rigid than when he walked away from her only a few minutes earlier. She pretended to scratch at her large, pointed teeth as she took the root into her mouth and tucked it under her tongue, then she let half her glamour fade, hoping to look more like a sea witch than a bog hag. Her intuition was nudging her to believe this place was a trap.

Wandering around the tables, she found her number across from a minotaur. Her least favorite meat, after cat or cat shifter. The stench of bull pheromones made her want to gag and she almost left but then she noticed three orcs and two ogres came in. The group hurriedly put on name tags and spread out around the tables without signing the registration book. They moved together like a mall of bears, bulky and thick, in the room filled with more petite creatures. Looking beyond her prey, she noticed Devlin holding a chair for a tittering siren. He was going to be popular with the younger witches and monsters who didn't know what vampires were meant to look like. As if sensing her watching him, he glanced up and gave her a handsome smile that should turn her stomach, but it didn't, it just made her pity him more. His eyes shimmered black.

She heard the vampire's whisper in her ear as though he were standing behind her. *"Don't drop your glamour. Something is very wrong here."* She nodded slightly.

"Do you know him?" Yuki asked. The yukinba or snow hag had immigrated from Japan a century earlier.

"My great-grandmother and his grandfather were allies in the dark years," Ewenoe answered. Glancing at Yuki's name tag she raised an eyebrow at the backward spelled word, Abnikuy.

"Never tell strangers your name." Her voice dropped to a whisper, "Something is wrong here."

"Arabella and I feel it too. Don't drink the beverages," Ewenoe warned, offering her last cat's claw root.

39

"Never do," Yuki refused it by closing Ewenoe's fingers over it like they were squeezing hands. "Be cautious, sister hag."

"You, too."

Ewenow noticed Yuki only let her glamour half-fade, so she did the same. It would be tiring but exposing her true self would not happen again and she hoped there wasn't an image of her when she showed Devlin what she looked like. The snow hag went to sit across from an ogre who watched Ewenoe with interest.

The bell tolled a funeral tone, so she turned to sit across from the minotaur who never looked away from her cleavage for the entire five minutes while he talked about his job as a farm hand at a local dairy. To keep from smelling him, she twisted her hair and played demure while she held the corded strand above her lips. She inhaled the scent of the swamp instead of gagging, then talked about singing to fish to lure them into nets for fishermen. Pretending to be interested until the bell tolled was like being stabbed with a pitchfork repeatedly. As he left, she nodded politely and wrote his name and contact number on her card. The next male was almost as unappealing.

She left her wine glass barely touched and was surprised when the fae bartender stopped at her table between rounds. "Would you like a different drink?"

Ewenoe tried not to look suspicious as she shook her head. "No thank you, it's lovely. I am just a slow drinker." She glanced around as a scarred werewolf sat down. He looked well-groomed, but she could smell flea powder and mange soap residue.

As the next round began, he introduced himself, "I'm Beta Rogan, and I'm looking for a pack witch." For the next five minutes, he talked about the pay and benefits, they seemed decent, but Ewenoe knew better than to work for wolves. Werewolves were arrogant and often pack witches were only paid enough to cover the cost of living on packed lands. Their alphas also expected to be obeyed without question no matter what they asked for.

"I'm sorry, I am not looking for employment. I have a job luring fish into nets with a fishery up the coast," Ewenoe lied, giving Audora Water's work history. She was glad her mold-green eyes and moss-green lips were similar to the seaweed coloring of a real sea witch.

Three more rounds passed, and three more males sat down and chatted before the ogre sat across from her. He glanced at her almost untouched wine glass then held up his beer stein. "A toast... to the most hideous hag in the room."

"To the thickest ogre in the room." Lifting her wine glass, Ewenoe took a small sip, making the root under her tongue turn bitter as the poisoned wine touched it.

Adjacent to them Devin staggered as he sat, his empty glass was replaced by the bartender. Ewenoe worried about how much he had drunk, with so many smells, she couldn't tell if he was intoxicated at a distance. She hoped the cat's claw didn't make him sick.

"I'm Kronk," the ogre introduced himself. "Pleased to meet you." He tapped his stein to her wine glass again, so she sipped a bit more as he said, "I've never met a witch who drank blood wine."

"My family had vampire friends before they were cursed with beauty. It's an acquired taste." She managed not to let her mold-green eyes slip to Devlin as she stated, "I feel sorry for them now. Once they were gloriously heinous and now, they look like human models rolled in glitter."

Kronk snorted. "I'm glad they were cursed. Leaves more witches for the rest of us." He belched as he finished his stein of something which smelled like black blood and lager. When he twisted to signal the bartender, Ewenoe saw a battle ax under his jacket. She knew what he was then because weapons were not allowed at these gatherings.

The fae bartender brought her another glass of blood wine with his fresh stein of black lager. "Cheers." He held the new glass out to her.

Several chairs down, Yuki began cursing at the orc across from her and threw a drink in his face.

Kronk chuckled. "She's spicy for someone who is supposed to be made of ice... Here's to no drama." His expression looked amused, but his beady eyes and scent were expressions of frustrated anger when she didn't take the glass.

Deciding she had enough of this game, Ewenoe eyed him. "Why are you trying to get me drunk on wine laced with witch's bane?"

His expression shifted from affable to aggressive. "What are you talking about?"

"I'm the kind of witch who smells things... like I can smell you're lying, and something else. Something you want to blame on witches."

"Just drink it so there won't be a problem," Kronk snarled then growled. "There's no sausage for your kind here."

Glancing at his hands Ewenoe noticed his nails were too clean to be a feral or clanless bridge dweller. Ewenoe smiled, showing all her pointed teeth as she flipped her tongue across the points. "Really? But I have a new recipe to try, traitor. I know what you ate for breakfast."

He stiffened, "What do you mean?" The commotion from Yuki's table was getting louder as she threw her chair at the orc before stomping away in a swirl of snowflakes.

"I have been to many meetings. I have never seen you, the other bridge dwellers, or the fake bartender fae before. There are also several males who could be warriors or enforcers who I haven't seen or scented

42

before." Ewenoe waved her hand around them. "So, because the invitation arrived the usual way, I would guess that at some point in the last moon cycle, the S.S.S. caught the old host and this whole party is a trap because of the missing children. We didn't eat them." Her hatred for him and what she knew he had done poured out of her eyes as her grin grew feral. "But I think you know who did."

He glared at her while the scent of his outrage crawled up her nose but then he smiled. "You have a wonderful imagination Audora of the sea." His expression was so opposite his scent that she ran her thumb over her ring. It felt thick and heavy as she turned it around. Her thumbnail unhooked the clasp which hid the paralytic-covered spike within, just in case he decided to attack her.

Chapter Four

The bell tolled, but Kronk didn't stand. Leering at her he said, "You're a tiny thing, sea witch, very hideous with wonderful assets. You won't be so cocky when you lose your magic and your teeth."

"And you're a meaty beast who wouldn't fit in any of my cauldrons, but that doesn't mean I won't try to cook you." She snapped her teeth at him. "Don't do this or you might lose something cocky that won't grow back. We witches know this is a setup."

At the sound of shattering ice, Ewenoe turned and noticed Yuki struggling against the orc holding her back. His feet were frozen to the floor. Suddenly, Kronk overturned the table and seized her in a headlock. His thick thumb forced her mouth open as he poured the tainted wine into it.

"Ewenoe!" Devlin shouted her real name as she bit off the ogre's thumb. Kronk roared in pain, releasing and shoving her to the floor before she could impale him with her ring.

43

Werewolf Rogan jumped on Devlin's back to stop him from interfering, but Devlin's vampire speed and strength allowed him to fling the mangy wolf away before he backhanded the ogre over his chair.

"Flee," Devlin ordered as he squared off with Kronk. He attacked the much larger ogre.

Choking on the wine, Ewenoe inhaled deeply then shouted, "It's the S.S.S., fight and flee, my sisters."

Chaos broke out in the ballroom. Monsters and witches began fighting the enforcers of the society that so oppressed every aspect of their lives while dozens of enforcers rushed out from hidden doors. The Fae bartender was in an all-out magic battle with Arabella, but the Voodoo priestess witch had the upper hand. The two fire witches she saw at the bar earlier, held hands as they burned the minotaur and a werebear with a blast of magic like a blowtorch. The orc who struggled with Yuki was shattered in frozen pieces scattered across the ornate rug, as the snow hag fought a wind mage wearing S.S.S. robes. It was obvious The S.S.S. agents counted on the tainted drinks laced with witch's bane to render the witches helpless. Magic of every kind collided and exploded. The room was filled with clouds of used magic dust, snow, ash, and smoke. The cacophony of bellowing monsters and screeching witches was deafening.

But Ewenoe couldn't worry about the mayhem at that moment, she had swallowed the cat's claw root when Kronk poured the wine down her throat. The bitterness mixing in her stomach made her projectile vomit at the feet of Kronk and Devlin while they battled. Wrestling, they slipped on the slimy mess. Falling, the large ogre landed on top of the smaller vampire.

Roaring an ogre battle cry, Kronk punched Devlin hard enough to break bones. "Time to die, Sparkles!" His giant hand clenched around

Devlin's neck. The vampire clawed at him.

Fearing Devlin's head was about to be torn off, Ewenoe punched the ogre in the side of the neck with her poisoned ring. The ogre yelped and swatted at her with his other hand. She seized his wrist with a strength that surprised him, biting off two of his thick fingers next to his missing thumb. Her sharp, shark-like teeth severed the joints easily. Jerking his arm away from her, his blood sprayed on her dress, cleavage, and face. Kronk's momentum carried him onto his back then he froze as the paralytic worked. Licking her lips, Ewenoe groped underneath Kronk and wrestled his battle axe free.

"Hang on, Duncan."

The ogre's eyes leaked tears as she hacked off his arm with one swing. Devlin clawed the hand paralyzed around his throat.

Standing next to the ogre as his blood sprayed out of the stump, soaking her to the skin, she snarled, "At least, I didn't cut off something that won't grow back, child eater." Then she stomped his manhood with her heavy oversized boot, as she stepped over him.

"We have to escape!" Ewenoe shouted over the noise as she dragged Devlin to his feet. With her other hand, she hit Kronk in the face with a small sachet that exploded with yellow powder. "Forget us!"

She started to pull Devlin toward the front, where witches and monsters battled the S.S.S. enforcers and mages, but he scooped her up in his arms like a bride and then everything went darker than a starless, moonless night. The dampness of dew-wet spider webs clung to her exposed face and arms. When the light returned, they were standing in the dark alley behind the building. Devlin panted and staggered, falling to his knees and dropping her. The thump of Kronk's arm between them surprised her but she quickly held the oozing end up.

"Drink before you pass out." She knew from Baba's memories;

shadow walking was the most dangerous and draining thing a vampire could do. It was a last-resort escape ploy.

She pulled his arm over her shoulder and hauled him to his feet as he sucked the blood from the severed limb. She guided him back to the sidewalk and looked up and down the street for her pebbles. Seeing the faint purple glow, she hurried to follow them and escape. The noise from the monster and witches' trap spilled into the street on the opposite side of the building. Screeches of witches, bellows of beasts, and the crackling of magic echoed. The stench of blood filled the breeze. The noise faded the further they got away from the warehouse. As they reached her house twilight began to fade into day. She realized a time slowing spell must have been cast on the entire venue. She hurried to get them inside as the sun broke the horizon. Devlin groaned in pain because the lighter it got the more he sparkled until wisp of glitter rose from his skin like smoke. They stumbled through the door, and she kicked it shut.

"Haggity, baggity, boggy, boe! Get up and walk; to the safety of the swamp we go!" Ewenoe incanted the words to turn her home from building to vehicle. The house began to rock as it walked away from the vacant lot.

"Get up, Drakul!" She ordered in the same tone her great-grandmother once used to get her out of bed.

Devlin only moaned and curled into a ball in front of the door.

Desperation leached into her voice as Ewenoe begged, "Get up... You have to get out of the light!"

Rushing into her bedroom, she seized a blanket from the bed, then rushed back and threw it over him. She rolled him up in it and dragged him into the bedroom. Shoving him into the closet, the darkest room in her house, before shutting the door, she stuffed rags around the frame. Going to the window she hung a second blanket over the tattered

46

curtains and dirty glass to block as much light as she could. Looking down at her vomit and blood-covered sundress, she realized her shawl was lost in their escape. In disgust, she threw her dress in the fire and put on a simple gray nightshift. She couldn't even bathe while her house was walking, or the tub would slosh water everywhere. The dried blood would have to wait.

Going into the main room, she saw Kronk's arm lying on the floor tied in Devlin's scarf and smiled a terrible smile. Devlin had carried the gruesome trophy all the way to her home despite his weakened state. He said he could love a witch who cooked from scratch, and it was time to start cooking. At the very least, she owed him a meal, so she put the ogre's arm in a dutch oven with apple cider vinegar, and put it in the coals of her stove. She needed to cook it long enough to peel off the skin.

Looking at Devlin's bloody scarf, she tried to peel the tag off, but it wouldn't come loose. Examining it closely, she realized it was bound to the woven threads by magic and there was a tracking charm on it.

Opening the window, she called a magpie and gave it the scarf. "Carry this far from my home. Away, away you go!"

Her house continued its steady pace away from the place that almost saw her captured and enslaved. Tiredly, she went to her room and lay on her bed. Belching, from the raw ogre fingers she swallowed, there was a flavor to the meat which could only come from one thing. As she fell asleep, she wished she had cut off Kronk's head when she had the chance.

Chapter Five

After her nap, she used her crystal ball to scry for the early evening supernatural news. The crystal ball reported, *"Early this morning, dozens of witches and monsters were arrested at an illegal mate-seeking meeting. The warehouse where the event was held burned to the ground when the witches attacked agents of the Supernatural Supervision Society without cause. There were several werewolf, werebear, orc and ogre enforcers injured. A minotaur captain, a fae agent, and two troll administrators were killed in the melee, along with fifteen witches and monsters who attended the illegal gathering. The S.S.S. is looking for a sea witch and a sparkly vampire who incited the riot. Here are their pictures. If you see...*"

She waved her hand over her crystal ball to silence it after their false names were given with pictures of Devlin and her glamour. She realized the pictures were taken at the registration table. She could hide as her true self but creating a new glamour would take months. She worried Devlin might never be able to be seen in public again because cursed vampires took centuries to change their appearance. Scratching at the dried ogre blood under her shift, she knew she would just have to keep him inside her house and keep moving.

As the recipe slowly cooked, the evening became night. Ewenoe carefully unpacked the torn cloth from around the door frame and opened the door to the closet. Devlin was still curled in a blanket. He moaned and hissed when she touched his shoulder.

"Devlin? It's Ewenoe... Are you restored?" she asked as softly as she could, noting the large number of sparkles sloughed off his skin onto the floor and blanket. His profile had become haggard, diminishing his beauty but making him more attractive to her. When he didn't answer, she gently prodded his shoulder again. She knew a hungry vampire, regardless of their beautiful curse, was still a very dangerous monster.

"Want more ogre blood," he muttered in guttural tones.

"I don't have any more fresh blood, only mixed blood preserved in jars in my..." Her breath caught in her throat when he suddenly leaped at her.

Pinned to the bed, she could only stare at him in shock as he crouched over her. His whole body seemed to be withering. Tearing her shift open, he began to lick the dried ogre blood off her skin. "Must... have... more. Must clean... off her."

Laying perfectly still, she let him continue, knowing better than to disturb the predator now grooming her. The rasp of his tongue scraping the dried blood from her body was thrilling. Eventually, he fell asleep clinging to her and murmuring, "Don't leave me. Please love me... You're so hideous and perfect... I'm sorry I'm sparkly... I'm sorry I'm ugly beautiful."

Ewenoe ran her hand through his perfect raven locks and was surprised when his hair came out in clumps, shedding onto the blankets and pillows with the sparkles from his skin. As she rubbed her hands over his bare flesh, it almost seemed like she was rubbing the curse off of him.

Withdrawing from his embrace before dawn, she felt her house stop. They were deep in the swamp, next to her bog under giant cypress trees. Standing at her door, she savored the scents. It was one of her favorite places to settle her house. After checking the stewing meat and peeling off the ogre skin, she went outside to gather medicinal plants and scooped up a bucket of sludge. Boiling the plants and some medicinal powders with the sludge, she only let it cool slightly. She smeared the smelly, warm paste on every bit of his skin to work like a drawing salve before she wrapped him tightly in the blankets and tucked him back in the closet. It took hours to sweep up the sparkles and curls of hair before she burned them, then she took a nap. At sunset, she unwrapped him.

"Ewenoe..." He moaned her name but did not wake.

"I'm here, drink this." She tried to get him to drink the preserved, thickened blood from a jar, but he squirmed, turning his head away. Frustrated, she went back to the kitchen and tried to think of what she could feed him.

The ogre meat was falling off the bones, so she separated it and shattered the bones to scoop out the marrow to feed him. She ladled some broth into a bowl and whisked in the marrow and a cup of black blood. Fevered and incoherent, he gulped the marrow, blood, and broth mixture, then went back to sleep. She put the cracked, empty bones over the fire to dry as she made him a bath. She coaxed Devlin awake and into a tub of boiled bog water to scrub the pasty sludge off. His change shocked her as she wrapped his naked body in clean sheets and tucked him into the dark closet to sleep the day away. Tiredly, she soaked the sheets and blankets with his clothes.

Pulling out a crystal shard broken from its sisters, she smeared a drop of blood on it and called, "Baba Yaga? Grandmother? Are you there?"

"Ewenoe, my sweet girl, why do you look so tired?" Her great-grandmother's eyes were sharp as a cat's peering at her through the shard. "Please tell me you weren't part of that nonsense in the city."

Ewenoe sucked in her moss-green lips. "I went looking for an ingredient... for perogies. I am slow cooking an ogre arm and drying the bones for flour."

Baba cackled with wicked laughter. "That always was your favorite growing up. It's a good thing you didn't get a leg. The thigh is very tough and stringy and has to be stewed for a week to make it edible."

"Grandmother, they are blaming the witches for the missing city children but it's the ogres. I smelled it on him and tasted the child's innocence in his blood when I bit off his fingers," she revealed. "I don't know what to do."

The wise old crone rocked back and forth thinking for several minutes. "First, you must report him to the Society, and if they do nothing, then you know what to do... You are a Yaga, a bog hag. We preserve the innocent and consume the wicked. If you do not think you can handle him alone, get your Snow Hag friend and that Voodoo priestess to help you. Their kinds have the same creed as we do."

"Yes, Grandmother, but I don't know if they escaped the meeting."

"If you need it, the family will come to help you deal with them. Nothing is more important than family, except saving the innocent."

Ewenoe saw her grandmother raise her hand to end the communication and called out, "Wait... There is something else. Do you remember Vlad Drakul's grandson Devlin?"

"Ahh, yes... Poor lad was born with that wretched Beautiful Curse. What of him?"

"We saved each other from the Society's trap, and I am hiding him here but... I think I may have found a cure for the curse." She carried the shard in and carefully entered the closet. Holding a candle above the sleeping Devlin, she heard the oldest living bog hag gasp as she moved the crystal shard over him.

"I never realized how much he looked like Vlad. Send me a scroll of everything you did. I need to verify it before I tell the high lord of the vampires there may be a cure for the Beautiful Curse... Oh, Ewenoe, I always knew you were bright... Don't forget to burn the ogre's skin. Once the meat is cooked and the bones are ground to flour, the S.S.S. will never know from whence it came. Enjoy your meal, my precious. I love you."

"I love you, Grandmother Baba."

The glow of the crystal faded, leaving only the candlelight to look at Devlin in. He lay as still as the dead in a tomb. Bending over him, she pressed her lips to his before going out again. After making her grandmother the scroll by writing on parchment in bog snail ink so no other species could read it, she sent it away with Baba's ebony gander when it landed in her boggy pond.

51

"Take this to Baba Yaga, you good goose."

The dark gander honked at her, then swallowed the scroll before flying away.

She watched the ogre skin slowly burn. Silently, she wished she could create dragon fire or had basilisk coals. Too keep busy so she wouldn't hover because a watched skin never burns. She went about hanging the laundry from a line tied between two cypress trees. Her cat hissed from the porch, and she saw a wolf watching her as it scratched at flea bites.

She pretended not to know him as she screeched, "Be gone, mongrel. I don't care for wolf stew!"

Going into her house, she debated on leaving but she knew fleeing would just make the wolf chase her. Wolves loved to chase females, especially females who wanted nothing to do with them.

She hurried to finish the perogies. First grinding the dried bones into flour and making dough, she rolled it as thin as four sheets of parchment and cut out the round. While the pasta rested, she peeled and half-boiled carrots and potatoes, and then chopped cabbage and onions to mix with the bits of shredded ogre meat. She liked her meat seasoned with wild garlic but did not know if Devlin was allergic or not, so she only added salt, pepper, paprika, thyme, coriander, and cumin. Nervously, she made the potato-carrot-cabbage-ogre perogies with practiced ease.

"Be calm... When they come, they will only find a bog hag and an old-world vampire having dinner. No crime, nothing punishable." She prayed to Hecate she was right.

There was still quite an amount of meat and gristle left so she ground it seasoned with rosemary, cumin, sage, salt, and black pepper, and stirred in half a preserved bottle of mixed, thickened blood before filling entrails to make black-blood sausages. It made her cackle, thinking about how she told the troll she liked thick orc or ogre sausages because the ones she was making were far larger than the one she stomped belonging to a certain child-eating ogre. She put the sausages in jars of brine and cider vinegar to cure and canned all but two of the thick sausages in a canning pot of boiling water. Boiling the last two sausages in a separate pot of water before she boiled the perogies, she started on dinner. The butter in the skillet sizzled as she browned the outside of the meat, then she sauteed the perogies. The smell made her mouth water and her overly large teeth ache with the need to bite something. She hummed happily as she finished the gravy for the meal.

"Ewenoe?" Devlin stood in the doorway in just a sheet. "What is that wonderful smell?" He looked so handsomely heinous with his pasty, corpse skin and lean muscles that she blushed puce.

"You're awake... Come and eat. I know your family line means you can eat meat and small amounts of other things," she encouraged as she generously ladled the gravy made from the last of the broth and bone marrow over the food. "The pasta is made with bone meal, not white wheat flour."

He held his arm over his chest in a self-conscious gesture because she kept glancing at him. "I don't know where my clothes are. Sorry about how I look."

"I'll get them." She went out, but decided to only bring his pants so she could continue to ogle him. "Sorry, the others aren't quite dry."

"Thank you." He smelled embarrassed and she wondered if he would be blushing if he could.

"Your other clothes and the blankets are drying on the laundry line. Dress quickly. I made black blood sausage and ogre perogies for dinner."

"It all smells amazing. Thank you." He took his pants and retreated to her bedroom.

Chapter Six

When Devlin came out, he just looked at his plate, so she put a fork in his hand. "Eat. before it gets cold."

After the first tentative bite, Devlin began to devour the food like a starving monster, while Ewenoe ate slowly, savoring every morsel as she repeatedly peeked at him. He had no idea how attractive he was to her now with his pointed teeth, hawk-like nose, sallow skin, and bald head. She thought his face was much better looking without his dark curls and eyebrows.

Catching her watching him, he looked ashamed as he asked, "Is there more?"

She stood and started toward the stove, but he stopped her, "I'll get it, you're still eating." He refused to let her serve him another plate and got it himself after putting more on her plate first, then asked, "Could... Would you ever date or mate a male like me?" When she raised her eyebrow, he gave her a smirky smile and shrug. "Well, you can't blame me for trying."

Giggling, Ewenoe admitted, "I would marry you after what happened the other night."

His flirtations quickly faded as he stared at her in shock, stammering, "But... But that was a dream."

"No, you licked the ogre blood off my skin, among other things." Smiling wide enough to show all her pointed teeth, she teased, "I may never let you leave."

"But I'm handsome, cursed... I freaking sparkle in..." Holding up his hand, he suddenly paused noticing the change of his flesh for the first time. Looking at himself, he began rubbing his hands over his arms and chest. "What happened to me?"

Getting up, Ewenoe dug in a chest hidden behind her couch for an enchanted mirror as she asked, "Why did you carry the ogre's arm outside with us after I cut it off? And all the way to my home as we escaped?"

"You save my life, and I figured the least I could do was save the reason you went there in the first place... it was absolutely delicious by the way. I never thought ogre would taste so amazing."

"I know," she said, accepting the compliment, "it is one of my great-grandmother's best recipes." She held out the mirror. "Look at yourself now."

"Devlin looked confused as he took the handle. "Vampires can't use mirrors."

This is a special mirror made by my great-grandmother Baba. It is a mirror for monsters. Lord Drakul once used it to see what he truly looked like after his change." She put her cold hands on either side of his face. "The curse is broken. You look..." Her breath caught in her chest with her hope for them. "You're a monster like he was. A true Nosferatu. The ogre blood cured you and a swamp sludge toxin-drawing mask removed those horrid sparkles from your skin. Don't be afraid, look at yourself."

Shaking as he looked into it, Devlin gasped. He touched his ears and opened his mouth, gaping at his fangs while one hand ran over his bald head, then he started laughing and crying at the same time. "I'm cured. You cured me." He pulled her into his lap and kissed her, careful not to cut his tongue on her pointed teeth.

A kiss was something she had never experienced. It made her lightheaded as her heart pounded. She felt like the world was shifting then she realized her house was moving. Jumping up from his lap, she rushed to the window and looked out. A pack of werewolves was chasing them and snapping at the cottage's chicken legs trying to carry them to safety.

"House, stop," she ordered knowing it was futile to run away.

Looking at Devlin, she revealed, "It's the S.S.S."

He nodded then reminded, "Devlin Drakul and Ewenoe Yaga weren't at the warehouse. They can't prove it was us." He caught her around the waist clutching the window frame as the house shifted kicking one of the wolves away from the door.

Wrapping her spare shawl over her haunch and shoulders, Ewenoe went to the door. "House, settle."

Opening the door, she stepped out into the cool midnight air, "I'm sorry my house is a little high-strung. What do you want?"

One of the wolves shifted and stood naked in the bog. She recognized him but schooled her expression into unimpressed curiosity.

"I am Beta Rogan of the S.S.S. Are you the sea witch Audora Waters?"

"No, I am Ewenoe Yaga, a bog hag. Why would you think I was some wretched sea witch?" she demanded as disdainfully as she could like she was offended he didn't know the difference between types of witches.

Devlin came up behind her wearing one of her loose peasant blouses. On him it looked like something the males of the old country often wore. When he stepped out the wolves backed up whimpering or growling.

"Who are y-y-you?" Rogan tried not to sound afraid, but Ewenoe could smell the werewolves feared Devlin.

"I am Lord Drakul, a Nosferatu vampire. Is there a problem? My beloved and I were just finishing dinner when you dogs scared her house?" His heavily accented voice was cold and yet powerful. It made Ewenoe tingle in all the good places. His next words vibrated the air, "This is not the witch you are looking for."

"This is not the witch we are looking for," the werewolves muttered as one.

Watching their dazed expression she whispered, "Can I ask Rogan a question?"

"Yes, he won't remember unless I tell him to," Devlin shrugged.

"Beta Rogan, if I were to report one of the S.S.S. ogre enforcers for eating human and witch children, what would happen to him?" She grimaced, showing her pointed teeth. There was one rule in the Yaga family which no bog hag dared break because Baba or Gretal would come for them: children are not food. It was the reason Gretel was forgiven and welcomed into the family after killing Great-grandmother Baba's sister, Orba.

"Answer her," Devlin growled in his unearthly deep tone.

"The enforcer would be reassigned," Rogan slurred.

"What about punished?" Ewenoe hissed. "He should be punished for eating children... And for blaming the witches. All those witches killed the other day were innocent."

"There is no punishment for enforcers other than reassignment," the dazed werewolf answered.

Devin put his arm around Ewenoe's waist to keep her from killing them all while he demanded, "Explain why."

"It is part of the bridge dwellers' immunity from prosecution agreement. If he were accused, he would only be reassigned to a new section with a warning and no investigation. If he is caught actually killing or eating a child, he would only be retired and allowed to return to his clan. ," Rogan growled as he said the words. She could smell that he didn't agree with the policy.

Devlin's grip tightened to keep her from tearing the wolves to pieces. "Calm down," he whispered in her ear. "We'll take care of Kronk ourselves."

Panting she let herself sink into the side of her monster. Devlin snapped his fingers. A moment later, Rogan and the other werewolves blinked at them.

"Sorry to interrupt your evening Lord Drakul, but there is a sparkly vampire and a sea witch we are looking for. They maimed an ogre enforcer in the riot the other morning."

"That's terrible," Devlin responded without revealing his contempt, though she could smell it.

"Is he recovering?" Ewenoe managed to almost sound sincere, but she would hate it if he still lived.

"His arm was hacked off and taken, but it will grow back. Have no fear, the enforcers of the Supernatural Supervision Society will find and detain these criminals," Rogan responded with false bravado. "Just like we did those other witches who were stealing children."

"See that you do and don't bother us again." Devlin used his tight grip to practically drag her back inside before she could start screeching at Rogan about why those witches were innocent. Over his shoulder, he gave the werewolves a curt, "Goodnight."

He kept his hand clamped over her mouth until he could no longer hear the heartbeats of the werewolves. Her teeth nipped at the meaty part of his palm but didn't break the skin. He was glad she chose not to bite his hand off.

"They're gone." He dropped his hand and then looked at her, "How did you know Kronk had been eating children?"

"I have my great-grandmother Baba's memories. She smelled it in her sister's house and in her meat after Aunt Gretel killed her. Child meat smells very different from adult meat and clings to the flesh of those who consume it," she looked up at him with her mold-green eyes. "You have to believe me."

"I do. The House of Drakul can read memories of those whose blood we drink. He and the one called Turk shared a toddler for breakfast the morning before the raid. My grandfather Vlad forbid harming children."

In their shared anger and outrage, he became more hideous and terrifying than any monster she had ever seen. She thought she might swoon when he ran his clawed nails along her cheek and rubbed his thumb over her lips.

"My beloved bog hag, I think I need to acquire you some more ogre meat and blood because I love your cooking almost as much as I love you."

"I love you too." Ewenoe grinned at him showing off her unnaturally wide smile and pointed teeth. "But only if I get to come with you and cut off something which won't grow back, and then we will begin curing your family from the Beautiful Curse, one child-eating ogre at a time."

Returning her smile, and showing off his impressive fangs, Devlin nodded, promising, "Anything you wish, my hideous hag, anything at all."

THE PRICE PAID
KARLA HAILER

Silly child
She came to me with a wish
Her heart's desire...

I tried to tell her
There are consequences,
A price to pay,
And it may not seem like much

But it is often higher
Then anyone thinks
     Until it's too late.

When souls are at stake,
The cost is always high.

So young and desperate
She begged
She pleaded
She promised and swore

Anything,
  Everything,
    Name my price.

He was rich and powerful
Who cared if he was only OK looking?

He would keep her in a lifestyle
Which she would like to be accustomed.

He would always support her
If she bore him a male child.

All I had to do was utter the word
And they would be forever bound.

Sending her away,
She spilled tears on sacred ground.

Begging me to reconsider.
Begging me to help her.

Turning my back,
I walked away.

But she grabbed my dress
Pleading for mercy.

"Dear child, I am showing you mercy."
I told her.

I tried to tell her,
Coming to me
  By definition

Means being so desperate
The stakes were higher than she realized.

"Name your price, it's yours."
She whispered.

Third time is the charm.
I told her I would name my price
When the time was right.

Bowing her head,
I granted her wish.

She accepted my spell then,
Happily, went her way.

They became bound
She bore him a son
Then had to watch as
Women came and
Women went.

Bound, but not loved.
Bound, but not respected
Bound and imprisoned
By her own blindness.

She came to me again
Careworn and broken.

Reason had abandoned her
But the old hag would not.

I tried to warn her.
No man was worth her freedom and dignity.

Innocents like her are easy to fool
With flattery and gifts
Now, she cried,
"Have I paid the price?"

"I do not ask for me,"
She cried out
"I beg for my son.
Do not make him pay
For my foolishness."

With a smile,
I uttered,
"Here are my terms.
You have agreed."

She hung her head as
I cast the spell.

May he be smart enough
To find the door
As the tides turn
Even as his mother
Pays the price.

Rising, she understood,
Her life was over,
His life was over,
But her son's would begin anew.

Picking up the silver dagger at her feet,
She bowed and gave thanks
For ending the terror
From which she blinded herself.

And I could transplant two more
Unfortunate souls
To grow in my gardens.

BEWARE THE BOG HAG
KATY MANZ

Chapter One

Jaxson

"And then the Bog Hag captured them, and they were never seen again."

"Flynn, stop scaring the children." I shook my head while comforting the poor preschoolers foolish enough to have begged their Papa Flynn for a nighttime story. "Seriously, I should make you take an extra turn at sleeping in their room tonight instead of in our room wrapped around our mate."

"Nope." Flynn rubbed a hand over his rounded belly, smirking. "A certain alpha somehow managed to knock up both of his omegas during the same month, so we omegas get to cuddle in the bed these last few weeks while Daddy Jaxson takes care of the older children. Love you."

The brat's laughter carried through the hallway as he joined Rhys in the bedroom and left me alone with the children.

"It's okay, Daddy." Our son Nouvel placed his little hand in mine. "I'll help you get everyone in bed. The Bog Hag doesn't scare me."

"No?"

"Nope." Nouvel shook his head, his expression serious. "Have you seen Papa Rhys when he's protecting his family? That old witch stands no chance against us."

Chuckling, I hugged my son. "You're right. Nothing can bring this family down."

Rhys

"The Bog Hag has gotten an unfair reputation. She would never just come and take one of the children." I changed out of my shirt from earlier and replaced it with my comfy sleep tee. "Why must people continue to tell these fables?"

"Because they are fun to tell around the spookiest time of the year?" Flynn plopped down on the bed and unbuttoned his pants. "Do we really need to wear pants for the next couple of weeks? Can't we wear long robes and just not leave the house?"

"That would be my plan if I didn't have to do this special favor for the council." I lay down on the bed and rolled closer to my mate. "Seriously, though, can you stop telling the kids these ridiculous stories? They are going to confuse facts and fabrication."

"Fine." Flynn leaned in and kissed me. Our large bellies blocking the way to holding each other closer. "But are you sure it's safe for you to visit Meredith in Swamp Loki by yourself? I could come with you. Or maybe Jaxson."

"Don't be silly. I have met with this region's Bog Hag and always returned safely. This time will be no different."

"Promise?"

"I promise. Now, go to sleep. You know these little guys will punch our bladders in two hours, so we'd better get rest while we can."

Chapter Two

Rhys

Surrounded by the putrid stench and burps of trapped air releasing, I was grateful for my sigils as they blocked most of the sensory overload. Rotting vegetation, hanging moss from the blackened branches, and swarms of insects welcomed me to Meredith's territory.

I hated visiting the swamp. Although I saw how the atmosphere was natural and a necessary part of our world, I needed less humidity and mosquitoes.

"Meredith," I called out to the witch who claimed this area as her own. She was warned I would be entering the borders. At least, she should have been.

"Rhys." The Bog Hag's hiss of my name snapped my attention to the eastern corner of the swamp, where I found her crouched over the petrified remains of a toad. "I was just practicing some old spells from my grimoire. If you don't use the skills, you risk losing them."

"It's nice to see you again." I stood where I was, waiting for her to invite me closer. Only once she gestured for me to proceed did I step within arm's length of Meredith. "I hope the Global Shifter Council contacted you and informed you of my visit today."

"We both know that if they hadn't, this would be going an entirely different way, Rhys." The powerful woman probably would have already skinned me for crossing her boundaries. Since I knew the rules, I would pay the consequences if I crossed without permission.

"True." I pulled out the small bottle the GSC had asked me to bring to Meredith. "Did Samuel detail the reason for my visit? I don't want to bother you with explanations if you are already informed of the situation."

"I appreciate that. I do hate wasting my time." Meredith snatched the bottle from my grasp and examined it. "I will look into the contents and meet with you in twenty-four hours to discuss my findings."

"I can return here—"

"No." Meredith's stare buried itself within my soul, her energy making its presence known. "Don't come back here. I will come to find you."

A sticky heaviness took over my body, and I stood frozen. She was testing my strength and magic. We had done this dance before, and she knew how powerful a magic weaver I was, but she had never seen me while I was pregnant. The child within me would carry its own power, and she couldn't help but test to see how much. Since I had experience with her, I knew we would be all right if I didn't fight and let her probe the energy. When I felt a slight sting from her force, I warned her. "Remember the treaty, Meredith."

"I'm aware of that document, Agent. I'm also aware of how far I can push it. I have what I was searching for anyway." Meredith's mouth stretched into a creepy mimic of a smile. "That little one will be a mighty witch, you know."

"I felt a surge in my energy source, so I figured she would be."

"He. He will be."

"The doctor said it would be a girl." I was sure the doctor was correct.

"Don't dismiss my vision, Rhys," Meredith warned. "That little wolf is an omega witch and has an exciting part to play in the future of shifters and magic weavers. If you need advice later about any powers he displays, message through the normal channels, and I'll reach out to you. Certain ancient ways want to resurface secret forms of energy that were lost in time. Your child will be the key to bringing them back."

I swallowed hard at the thought of this prophecy's heavy weight on my son. But I was more worried about what was in this for Meredith. She did not offer help for free. Even the GSC had to pay her a steep reward for her contributions to our research. But she was one of the most powerful beings around, and, sometimes, we needed that force. "Why would you help me?"

"I wouldn't." Meredith's cackle sent a chill down my spine. "But when I feel a presence even more powerful than I am in a soul still so new, I can't help but want to be close."

"You will not take my child." I'd heard the stories but hadn't seen proof that the Bog Hag stole children and other humans, gaining the label of evil beings. I knew that all things could be seen as evil or good depending on who viewed them. And I knew that legends didn't always paint the truth. But something told me I needed to be wary of Meredith regarding my child.

"Of course not." The Bog Hag lifted a crooked finger and pointed toward the exit of the swamp. "I think it's time for you to go now, Rhys. But I will see you again very soon."

Chapter Three

Flynn

"I don't like the way she threatened our child." Jaxson stormed out of the bedroom, and I soon heard the clang of dishes. Our alpha mate had developed the habit of doing chores when frustrated and unable to act on his desire to protect us. I would not complain when the outcome was a clean house and our mate not getting into trouble with the GSC for ruining a treaty or being skinned alive by the Bog Hag. I shivered at that thought.

"He does realize that there is no way in hell you would let anyone near our child if they had negative intentions, right?" I turned and found Rhys shaking his head and laughing at our overdramatic mate.

"I swear he took on all our mood swings this pregnancy. He has been so emotional lately, and, last night, I caught him in the kitchen eating cake frosting out of the pantry container." Rhys sat down on our bed and sighed. "I don't think we can dismiss Meredith's attention for our child, but I also don't think she would stand a chance against all of us and the pack."

"I agree." I sat beside him and wrapped him up in a side hug. "We should keep the kids inside while she drops off the information tonight though."

"It's Halloween," Rhys pointed out. "Why don't you and Jaxson take the children trick-or-treating with the rest of the pack kids? I can wait here for her to come. Perhaps Alpha Abraham will come by and sit with me. He will keep her from overstepping the bounds of the treaty."

"I can live with that." I kissed my mate on the cheek and stood up. "I better go help Jaxson and get the kids dressed and ready. The pack's meeting at the main house in an hour to go out as one large group, so I don't want to miss them."

"I'll call Abraham and tell him to let his mates know you are heading over there in a bit. And I'll ask him to come be my backup."

"Thank you." I pulled a protection satchel out of my pocket and tossed it at Rhys. "Keep this on you. The kids and I made them earlier. They said it is extra special because the sigils were particular to the Bog Hags."

"I told you to stop talking to the kids about those stories." Rhys chuckled and put the satchel into his pocket. "But thank them, and I will keep it on me."

Rhys

"I just felt a breach of our territory. I would say she should reach the house in five minutes." Abraham sat in the swing next to me and drank

73

hot apple cider. "I'm glad all the children are out of the pack lands. If she were interested in this child, who's to say she wouldn't find many of the others' abilities equally tantalizing?"

"Agreed." I looked out into the dark night and tried to sense her presence. But, so far, it had been quiet and still.

"Do you really think she would try something?" Abraham checked his phone and sent a text to his mates. "I told the group to stay away for a bit longer."

"I don't believe she would purposely betray her agreement with GSC, but I also don't want to test it."

"Alpha Abraham. Rhys." Meredith crept out of the woods across from my house and made her way to my porch, stopping at the foot of the stairs. I wasn't planning on extending an invitation to come farther onto our property.

"Hello, Meredith." Alpha Abraham stood and stepped down from the porch to greet our visitor. "I am just visiting with Rhys while the pack is out for the evening. I hope you don't mind."

"No need to lie, Alpha." Meredith smirked. "Rhys is not foolish enough to trust me completely, especially in his delicate condition. I respect him more for it."

Chapter Four

Jaxson

"Rhys is going to be mad we didn't stay with the rest of the pack." Flynn walked beside me, holding our youngest as our older children walked a few steps ahead. "And Abraham is probably going to give us a hard time for leaving his mates out there without letting them know we were heading back."

"Daddy, look." Nouvel stopped walking and pointed ahead of us to our house. "There's someone there with Papa and Alpha Abraham. I think Papa needs our help."

"Nouvel, come here." I crouched down and pulled my children close. "Your papa was meeting with the Bog Hag tonight—"

"The Bog Hag?" Nouvel's head swiveled back toward the group standing outside our home. "Then, Daddy, we need to go help Papa."

"We don't want her to know about your powers, Nouvel," I whispered and looked each of my kids in the eyes. "Can we put a shield over us so she can't sense the energy you children radiate?"

"Too late for that." The cackling from Meredith reached my ears, destroying my hope that we could get past her without her sensing the children's abilities. "I see that the unborn pup isn't the only special one in the family."

"Leave our children out of this, Meredith." Rhys straightened his shoulders and stared at the hag. "You gave us the answers the GSC were looking for on the spell. I think it's time for you to head back into your own territory."

"I'm unsure if I should leave when so much power is present here." Meredith walked closer to my children, and I pulled them behind me, along with Flynn, who was trying to go forward. He probably planned to take down the witch with his bare hands. I couldn't let him get hurt.

"Stay aware." A booming voice caused me to turn and look at my children, shocked to find that Nouvel was speaking. "You will leave the pack borders now, Hag, or you will forfeit all your powers to the youth of the pack."

"And who are you to threaten me?" Meredith stopped approaching us but didn't take her eyes off our son.

"I am your downfall if you do not heed this warning. The Moon Goddess has blessed our generation, and our future is not yours to decide."

"I see." Meredith turned toward Rhys. "I will offer my assistance if you need it in the future, but it seems that the Goddess has spoken through your son, and even I am not powerful enough to go head-to-head with such energy. Tell the GSC that the spell they are working with should be untraceable and unbreakable now."

"I will let them know, and your payment will arrive by the weekend."

"Much appreciated." Meredith turned back to Nouvel. "Your children are much more powerful than any of you have imagined. Be careful who you let into your territory, Alpha. Not everyone has a treaty with the council. Guard these kids with your life."

"We will," Abraham growled. His wolf, still feeling threatened by our visitor, wanted her off our land. My wolf communicated with him telepathically and agreed.

Without another word, Meredith slinked back into the woods, and I soon felt her presence exit the bounds of the pack lands.

Once we were safe, Rhys ran off the porch and gathered the children nearby. "I was so scared."

"Don't worry, Papa." Nouvel patted his father's cheek. "The Goddess wouldn't let the hag get to us. She told me last night what I would need to say and do if she tried anything."

"You spoke to the Goddess?" Flynn knelt and hugged our son.

"Yes. I talk to her whenever she has a message for us." Nouvel turned to Alpha Abraham. "We need to reinforce the magical boundaries. The hag was correct when she said others would be coming after us."

"I'll start that in the morning." Alpha Abraham shook my hand and started toward the main house. "Get some rest tonight. It looks like we have a lot to do in the morning."

"Don't worry, Alpha." Nouvel lifted his head and met our alpha's gaze. "We can overcome anything if the pack stays together. Trust the pack."

"I will, Nouvel." Alpha Abraham waved and returned to his house.

"Let's get inside and get ready for bed." Flynn motioned us to the house. "I think we have a big day tomorrow."

"Oh yeah." Nouvel took Flynn's hand and smiled. "The babies will be coming tomorrow night, too."

"What?" Rhys picked up our daughter and carried her inside the house. "Both babies?"

"Yup." Nouvel placed his shoes in his cubby next to the door and headed toward the stairs. "Don't worry. Their births will be easy. The Goddess told me to tell you to get some rest tonight. The babies aren't going to be great sleepers."

As our kids headed upstairs to start their bedtime routine, I hugged my mates and kissed their heads. "Don't worry, mates. We've done this before."

"I know. I just really like sleep." Flynn squeezed us tighter.

"We all do." Rhys giggled. "But we can do this. We can do anything. As long as we do it together."

CREATION
Devon Gambrell

Wiping the blood from her mouth, only to realize it too was covered in blood.

She gagged on the metallic tang when a clawed hand entered her blurred vision.

"Only two more to go, Little Hird."

Tears slipped down her cheeks. Mixing with the dripping blood. Accepting the leathery hand, careful not to touch the poisoned talons.

Goddard lifted her to shaking feet. When she couldn't hold her weight, he lifted her. Cradling her to his broad chest.

"I don't want to change," Hird whimpered into his chest, staring into the dark gloom of fog and scattered decaying trees.

"You want revenge, do you not?" his low voice rumbled his chest. "That is what you asked."

"I did not mean to turn into, this, thing." Hird touched her stiffened face.

"Power comes with a price, Little Hird. I cannot take back what you have promised."

Hird bit her lip as Goddard stepped over a fallen tree. His foot squelched into the swamp. She felt him sink into the muck. Just a little. He continued on.

The boy did not deserve to die; she thought with a sinking heart, and a hand over her mouth to stifle the cry that threatened to escape.

"His death will lure the ones you seek. And once you have tasted their flesh, your vengeance will be satiated," Goddard rumbled as if hearing her thoughts.

"And what will happen to me? Will I die as I should have done?"

"Nay, my Little Hird." It came out as a chuckle. "You will join the others. And when your powers are complete, you will join my family. We will protect our home and feast on the flesh of the diseased."

He stopped, his head tilted. "They have come to search for the boy."

Goddard needn't have said a word as her blood turned hot. Darkness that once blurred her vision turned to daylight as she turned her head to the intruders entering their home. Strength returned as Goddard gently lowered her into the squelch. Hird looked up at the giant. Limp, decaying reeds hung from his head, the moisture dripping down his hardy arms and legs into the sludge. His horns glistened with dew, yellow eyes regarded her.

"Be sure they know of their sins." Goddard sank slowly into the mud.

Her heart raced, her chest rose and fell as the shouts came closer, calling the child's name.

"That face doesn't suit you," Goddard said when he reached eye level. Hird touched the stretched skin of the child's older sister. Casting her eyes down in shame when his finger lifted her chin. "'Tis a simple matter to find another, Little Hird. This one will suffice for now."

Hird laid her hand gently in his, her hand wrapped around one finger, a small smile playing on her green lips. No longer mourning the death of the boy, she turned toward the shouts of the struggling humans. Goddard disappeared into the muck.

They are damaging my gardens.

SACRED FIRE
CASS VOIT

It had been two hundred years since the last time she courted someone. The loneliness was crippling. It made her feel like an Old Maid, because of her apparent age. She stopped her own aging at thirty years old.

She was the town witch and midwife, and not only did she help with pregnancies and births, she often cast love spells for the lovelorn. The fireplace was cold and dry, littered with charcoal and ash from the previous fire. The previous fire had been devoted to a client's spell, but this new fire was a special one: it was one for herself.

The temperature outside dropped slowly over time, and the cold began seeping into the house. It was not only time for a fire to warm herself by, but time for some spellwork.

She pulled the broom from the fire accessories and swept the ashes into a plastic bag, but she kept some of the charcoal on the floor of the fireplace to aid in the building of a new fire. This would be a sacred fire, one that would carry her intention to the gods.

A mix of birch and cedar lay waiting to the right of the fireplace in its own wrought iron basket. She stacked the wood, and she sparked the flame from the lighter in her hand. The single flame licked at the newspaper under the grate, and she stepped back to let the fire come to life. The flames spread quickly, Yellows, reds, and blues slithered and licked across the wood from the inside out, and the fire roared to life.

Whilst she warmed herself by the sacred fire, she closed her pale green eyes as she focused on her intention. She wanted someone male, someone tall and strong, and absolutely obsessed with her. On handmade paper, with imbued ink, she wrote those requirements down. The metal tip of the quill scratched against the paper while it distributed ink the color of coagulated blood in the shape of cursive. She ended the letter to the gods with "Someone loves me." She dropped the note into the center of the square. She watched in meditation as her intention singed and curled in the budding flames.

Suddenly, there was a thud that shook the oak door, causing her to jump and drop her quill on the floor, leaving what looked like a blood spatter in its wake.

She blinked at the silence, expecting another attack on the door. Her prophecy of another door wracking thud was fulfilled. While she had expected the next thud, she still jumped at the violence. The second attack caused a crack in the wooden door. She picked up her sword and slowly walked to the door and turned the knob tentatively, the door chain still engaged. On the other side of the cracked door, there was a giant wolf that wagged its tail upon being noticed. The wolf's tongue lolled to one side of the maw.

She closed the door so she could undo the chain and let it hang from the door frame. Opening the door again, wider this time, she looked the wolf straight in the eye. The memory that that's a big no-no for engaging with predators. The dire wolf tilted its head at her. She continued her cautious walk towards the wolf. "Did you break my door? What is it?"

Once she was in range, the wolf sniffed her hand and licked it. She took the invitation to pet the wild animal. Her slender yet unmanicured fingers glided through the fur on the top of the wolf's head between the ears. The wolf's muscles jerked, and she wondered if the lick was not an invitation at all, so she took an anxious step back away from the wolf.

Now that she had a fuller view of the massive wolf-dog, she saw its muscles moving under the black fur. Her eyes grew wide as the paw toes grew long, nearly human length, but bigger. The shoulders dislocated, and the wolf made a sharp yiping cry and crumpled onto the floor as the shoulders repositioned themselves. It writhed on the floor as the furred skin split, blood leaking onto the porch floor. Worried sick, she coaxed the wolf into the house.

She ushered the inexplicably wounded wolf towards the sacred fire, and she scrambled around the kitchen for her first aid kit to treat the new splits in the wolf's skin. She came back to a wolf convulsing on the floor, the splits showing new black fur growing in the slits.

She covered her mouth as she realized it was a he, taking shape in something resembling a tall, strong man covered in fur. The dangerously large maw of the changing wolf was clenched, bearing the sharp teeth in a fit of pain as it appeared that bugs were crawling under his skin all over his head. Eventually, the metamorphosis stopped and the naked wolf-man stood up and straightened his back. Oh, he was tall and strong alright, though she was sure he had a human form. She didn't want to think about what it would take to get to that form if it was even possible.

He towered over her. Covered in blood, the wolf-man stepped in close and tried to put his chin on her head, but she ducked out of what she thought was a limit on his range. His arms were longer than she expected, and large hands with large claws grabbed her by the upper arms, pulling her close. She struggled in his grip, but he picked her up off her feet, nuzzling her neck. She swallowed the knot forming in her throat. He was smearing his blood all over her neck. She continued to struggle, failing to avoid the bloody nuzzling.

It was then that she looked down at the floor and realized that her rugs were ruined.

The wolf-man must have taken her momentary stillness as consent, and his lipstick unsheathed itself. Her scream was silent as she choked on it out of anticipatory terror.

At that, the wolf-man pulled back to look at her and bared his teeth in a growl as he breathed into the side of her face.

It was time to do something. Anything. Anything but what he wanted.

Not want. No. He clutched at her and gave her face a long lick, teeth still glinting in the firelight. She shut her eyes tight. Despite everything in the past ten minutes, she realized she still had the lighter in her grip.

Perfect.

She brought the lighter to his chest and struggled to strike it to life. Click. Click click. FWOOM. The blood dampened the flame, and tears streamed down her face as he yipped and dropped her. She grunted loudly as she fell on her hip wrong. She pulled herself towards the fire and grabbed the fire poker from the fire accessories. Using the poker, she jabbed it behind a burning log in the front of the fire and pulled.

The log flew into the air. The wolf-man was too busy trying to beat the smoldering embers in his chest fur to notice the burning log flying toward him. It crashed into his jaw, dislocating his massive jaw.

Bigger dogs die young.

He yelped so loud that it hurt her ears as his face fur caught fire.

He howled as he clawed at his face. She took the opportunity to run. She had intended to sprint to the door, but she'd forgotten about her hip as she attempted to pull herself to her feet. She limped toward the door as he thrashed, the fire spreading to the dryer parts of him. He swung blindly towards her, and she screamed as she slammed her body into the door to avoid him. While she didn't remember closing it, the door closed itself on the regular. She jerked the door open and ran. It took everything she had to not crumple into a bloody pile on the ground in her attempt to flee her property.

She turned around when she ran out of breath.

Her house was ablaze.

Fuck. She didn't know what to do. So, she did nothing.

His painful howl pierced the night. She rubbed the bruising forming on her upper arms with her numb hands, trying to warm herself in the cool night. The lighter was missing; she had dropped the lighter at some point. "Never cast another love spell ever again" chanted in her head. She watched her life burn to the ground and simply stood in shock.

This taught her never to be selfish during a spell again.

THE BOG OF DAUGHTERS
SAM WICKER

Voracious wasn't the correct term, was it? She tapped her fingers on the rough bark of a red chokeberry, then caressed the colorful white petals nearby. One hand and half of her face felt the humid air while the rest of her body stayed cool in her aquatic domain. Prolific might be the word she searched for. A bee buzzed nearby before settling on another cone-shaped collection of pink flowers. Her companions for the past few decades were naught but the flora and fauna of the bog.

Until they moved in; the prolific ones.

Sitting on the outskirts of her watery domain, a house of white threatened to dominate. One man, eight women, three dogs, two cats, a screeching white bird, and some cattle. Building the two-story monstrosity took time. Every night she explored it, cleaning up her watered footprints upon the wood after curiosity faded. Eight bedrooms, six baths, a kitchen, a dining room, a living room, a den, an office, a small library, and a mudroom. The garage that held two cars stood next to the house, connected by a small covered walk, while the fenced in barn of deep red hunkered half a mile away.

She treaded water, slowly making her way to the edge of the fields. A cow lifted her head, chewing, and watching. Pulling herself up out of her watery land, she wriggled her toes in the sphagnum moss before walking to the cow. She rubbed the soft neck covered in curly brown fur, allowing herself the small pleasure of befriending another animal. "I am Rasa. You are?"she whispered, giving one last pat. She couldn't eat this one. Humans were particular about their livestock. Pets. She licked her lips, tasting the remnants of her last meal of slimy salamanders and tough goose.

Perhaps it was time to take her place among the humans again.

She smiled, walking lazily toward the house. Inhabitants crowded the kitchen and dining room, eating their first meal of the day while loudly complaining about the early heat. Summer in the bog was ripe with humidity. It was unbearable in the beginning for those new to the area. Humans quickly got used to many things. They were the best adaptors she'd witnessed in her long life, except for her kind.

Pale green, supple flesh, hair that appeared to be always wet and black in color, and of little weight. Once her kind were gorgeous, as they were thought of as goddesses. Now, the people believed them to be wart ridden, humpbacked things to be feared. She was somewhere in between. The humans that knew of her often thought she was an odd human woman, swamp bound, and lonely.

One thing the people got correct... she needed human skin to keep the populace from hunting her down and burning her at the stake. If they still did that. Did they? Pausing, she questioned the wisdom of her decision. Fire and she never got along.

Her green eyes swept out over her domain. Safe. Gathering

herself, she smiled and straightened her spine. She was about to have a family again. She waited and watched, pressed against the corner of the house, beneath a white oak's shade.

The youngest daughter of four was the first to escape the breakfast table. Running out with a giggle, she held her fluffy stuffed dog high as the smaller, equally fluffy, living dog barked and bounded beside her. The door slammed, bounced, then settled with a soft groan.

That one would not do. Not at all.

The mother pushed the screen open, "Jenny, please don't let the door slam again!" The woman shaded her brown eyes with a slender hand as she followed her daughter with her gaze. "Lord, it's already too hot." She huffed, using her other hand to wave air toward her face and neck, little brown curls waved back at her fingers in their escape from the messy bun. Her legs were bare under a pair of cargo shorts, and the t-shirt she wore had some brightly colored band logo.

"Mom! We're off!" A cry from the front of the house, the garage perhaps, as a car chuckled to life before the engine smoothed into its low purr.

"Be careful! Vic! Call when you get there! I know you've already forgotten the list." The mother turned, her words forced over the roof of the garage in a strained yell.

"I'll tell him, Mom." The grumble sounded through the yell in reply before a car door slammed.

She listened to the car wheels on the gravel, the sound fading with the distance before disappearing completely once the car entered the small strip of a forested area before the paved two-lane broke it up. She kept her eyes on the mother. Alone, with the tiny one, and the smaller dog. She assumed the other two and the cats were still indoors. There was one thing that made her hesitate.

What was the woman's name?

She heard her called 'mom', 'hun' and 'babe'. That was it. She couldn't call her one of those.

Frowning, she shrugged her worry off like a wet blanket and stepped away from the corner of the house. She watched the child disappear behind the barn and smiled. "Hello." Her voice felt like swallowing frogs.

She whirled, one hand at her collar bones, the other shielding her eyes from the sun. "Oh! Oh, you gave me a fright. Are you alright?" The mother's gaze swept up and down her, worry creasing her smooth brow over her hand.

"I'm sorry. I didn't mean to startle you." She smiled, not moving any closer, but rubbed her hands together in the way nervous humans usually did, "You see, there is a path between my house, nigh two miles that way, and my next neighbor's. I didn't realize this bit had been sold. Sos I just wanted to ask if'n you're alright with me passing through to see them?" She pointed to the east, where she knew there was another house that fit her description.

"Oh. Well, that's fine." The mother swallowed, looking toward the west, "But that house is about five miles, isn't it?"

"By the road, yes ma'am." She smiled again, "But the path shortens it a bit. Makes it about two, a little more. It's a pleasant walk. Since ya'll are new, you can come on over if'n you ever need anything.

See the path there? Just follow it, and...well, you have a car." She giggled, "It'll be the next mailbox."

"We'll do that. You do the same." The mother glanced toward the barn as the little dog yapped while the girl giggled behind it. "Want some tea?"

"I wouldn't want to intrude."

The mother waved her hand in dismissal, "No matter. I was gonna have some, anyway. Come on in, get some cool air."

She followed the woman inside, holding the screen so it wouldn't slam as she took in the interior. It differed from the rough foundation she'd explored. Everything looked polished, bright and white, with a mixture of frills and stainless steel appliances. The scent of the long gone breakfast lingered in bacon grease cooling in the pan.

"Oh."

She looked up, following the woman's sharp gaze down to her feet. "I see. I'll clean it up." Rasa lifted her head, smiling at the mother before lunging. She fell on the woman, pinning her against the porcelain double sink.

Her fingers slid into the woman's mouth, holding her still and quieting her. The woman couldn't avoid swallowing the essence of the bog from her body. Her magic. She poured it into the woman until her orifices leaked murky water. She couldn't wait for the last heartbeat.

Sliding a long nail under the mother's ear, she slit open the skin and began the actual work. Cutting down the base of the skull, she smiled as she recalled what her own mother called it. A backwards smile.

The woman's hair was nice and thick, it would hide the skin opening well.

At last, the heartbeat stopped. She let the body slide to the floor, taking the clothes and folding them neatly on the table. Taking in the scent deeply, cotton on a breeze, that brought back memories. These new smelly inventions were wondrous. Peeling the skin around the skull was the trickiest part. It was terribly easy to stretch the flesh, making it look odd to loved ones. Or to have an odd hang or snag somewhere that usually took too long to heal. The best part about skinning a human was pulling the skin from the fingers and toes. It was fun. Like taking off the gloves of a lover.

Once the skin was off, she lay it over the back of the kitchen chair. Tapping a bloody finger on her bottom lip, she looked over the rest of the mother. "I don't have time for any of that. What to do this time? It's been a while since someone has been missing, yes?"

Rasa nodded, answering herself. Stretching her fingers wide, she ran her hands over the muscles and tendons, swallowing them whole in slurps as the bones popped in and out of her body. Her magic deposited the mother somewhere in her bog. She would find it later, when she had the time and energy. Again, the skull was irritating.

Holding the skull in her hands, she poked at the eyes. Human eyes were still squishy. Hearing the laughter of the child reminded her of her limited time. She pushed the skull through herself, groaning at the bloated feeling before it forced its way out. Reaching for the skin, she stepped into it. Shimmying, she felt it snap into place at each bend. Rasa fisted her hands, then slid her fingers between each other, making the skin flush. Taking a deep breath, she pulled the face over hers, careful not to close her hair into the backwards smile, she fit the skin, pinching the opening closed. Like a bag the humans like to use to preserve things.

She preserved things, too.

Mavis. Mavis Ward. "How quaint," Rasa hissed as the skin reformed her body. Her magic took most of the pain, but the little pinpricks between bones annoyed. The warmth from the skin helped ease the discomfort, too. Like being wrapped in a hot towel. "Mavis for songbird and Ward for Marsh. Fitting."

Mavis began humming, cleaning the gore and bog water from the floor, the cabinets, and the chair.

"Momma! Look what I found!" Jenny grinned, holding up a frog as big as both of her hands put together. The little fluffy dog, Goldy, barked happily beside her.

"Why! Little Jenny, you know not to bring Mr. Frog in the house! It's a pretty thing. Best put it back in the bog before you get warts on your fingers." She grinned, chasing the little girl and dog back outside, giggling as the girl squealed.

###

Mavis adored her husband. If she'd been alive, there would probably be another daughter. Waters did nothing for suckling babes and neither did Rasa's womb. The mother's skin began revealing some wear and tear after two years. At the next holiday gathering, Mavis whispered some things to Jeridan's husband. Pointing out the grand endowments of Victoria, Jeridan's best friend in her sweet, motherly fashion. How could Victoria still be single? Why, the child practically bounced along with every boy she came across, but none of them stuck.

Jeridan walked in on him and her best friend a few months afterward.

She came crying back to her mother and father. Despite her young age, the mother passed away from old age after a few months. Heartbreak broke her of ever finding true happiness. Being the eldest, she took it upon herself to watch over the youngest ones, and her father. A mundane living. Friendless. Mateless. Her father, a shell of himself without his Mavis. As was she, without her best friend and love. Her meat tasted of depression and the ash of defeat.

The second, Dani, joined the navy, skipped, and the magic helped her take the third, Kaylie. Fitting into college for a month to withdraw after it became 'too much, with her sister dead,' was enough to drive anyone crazy. How humans dealt with the inane lectures was beyond her ken. Poor, poor Jeridan committed the worst sin, according to the book Kaylie loved. She'd never forgive her sister.

They found the mother in the fourth year after her disappearance, eight years after her death at the Rasa's hands. Mummified in the way bog waters do to humans. Rasa'd never had a chance to find Mavis' remains and make sure they were taken care of properly.

Still, it gave closure to the father and children. She didn't have to pretend to wonder where her mother had gone. Why she had left. And all those things humans go about when a loved one is missing. Kaylie was a marvel at that, staring out into space, lost in her mind. After three years of being lost in her own mind, Rasa grew quite bored. That car never slowed down. Kaylie's body smashed beyond recognition.

It was a challenge to remove tar from one's hands. Creating tire tracks was tedious, but worth it. Despite everything, Rasa was grateful for her large family, who she could go back to and continue living with. There was too much glass, too much smoke in Kaylie's flesh before the coroner filled it with that nasty chemical that killed all things.

The second finally came back, and she could slide into a mature body. Rasa had nothing to do with Dani's discharge from the navy. Her magic wasn't that strong. Luck. Pure luck. With Dani's skin, she was strong. With her honeyed-sun-kissed meat like oranges in her belly, she revived. Challenged everything and everyone. Racing along the paved roads. Flying through the bog waters, dodging roots and patches of land. Until the last day. She lost her life racing in the bog against Sasha, the fourth daughter.

As Mavis, Jeridan, Dani, and Kaylie, Rasa lived a full three years with each of their skins. Sasha... that child was different. When Rasa took her, Sasha said between gurgling breaths, "I knew it. I knew Dani wasn't Dani." Sasha would not be Sasha anymore, either.

At twenty-eight, Sasha still had a full life to lead. Rasa found it difficult to run Sasha's business of cosmetics and tanning beds. Southern women were strange in their necessity for the fake sunlight. She refused to clean and soon shut down. Sasha returned home and stayed home.

"I've got to take care of you, Daddy. Don't I?" Rasa said with Sasha's smile. She watched with the same smile plastered on her face as his red-rimmed eyes rolled, and he took another drink from the long-necked bottle. At this rate, he would die before she could survive in the younger ones' skins. Human livers were a weak organ, but tasty if not marinated in drink.

Two cops kept circling, talking nonsense in their slow drawls.

Strange how men sought to pin men in the deaths of women. Not that she could blame them.

As she fussed about the living room with its plush cushioned furniture in navy blue, and oak tables and stands, she drifted. Her thoughts rambling through her life. Since taking the mother, she had eaten no other humans. Her palate was satisfied with the Wards, their pigs and cows. Rasa mused she was getting old for such little meat to keep her sated.

The five bottles in her arm clanked as she straightened from picking up a sixth one. "Daddy, you're too young to be like this. I know it's been hard, but... we gotta still do." She let Sasha's brown eyes dig into him like daggers, "I shouldn't have to do this. You're only forty-three. Or is it forty-four now?"

"Go to work. Leave me alone."

His voice held little in it. Emotion lost to him now, as Vic's wife and children fell one right after the other. Four remained. Rasa hid her smile by swiping her nose with the back of her hand, three if we're being honest. "The salon closed, remember?" She added a dash of bitterness to the sentence, seeing if it would jab.

It didn't.

She strode into the kitchen, dissatisfied with the reaction from the only male figure in the house. Dropping the bottles in the trash, she cursed and dug them back out. Stepping outside, she put them in the blue bin instead. Overflowing bin. She put her hands on her hips, just like Mavis had, and pondered the wonders of modern recycling. Rather, the lack thereof.

"Jenny!" she called, "I thought you took the recycling yesterday?"

The leaden sigh wafted from the upstairs window down to her. Jenny's room hadn't moved since she was a child, a smaller bedroom dressed in greens and blues, right over the kitchen. Humans took too long to grow up these days. She remembered a time, only a few decades ago, where one of Jenny's age would be married and taking care of the house. Not huffing and sighing like a toddler fighting naps.

"Take it today," she pushed the door open, "Please!" She better be nice. Sasha was nice. Opposite of Dani. Sasha was also a push-over, but smart. Too smart.

"You're next, you know?" Jenny stated, pausing in her stomping stride to narrow her brown eyes, dark enough to be black in some lights, at her.

She stared down at the youngest in the kitchen. Not too long ago, she'd taken her mother in the very spot she was rooted to now. While Jenny was out playing. "I'm next for what?" Rasa made fists at her sides, Sasha's body trembling, "Don't. Don't you dare say what I think you're gonna say. That's..." she sniffed, "How could you?"

Jenny's eyes narrowed, sweeping up and down the body of her sister before looking back into their matching eyes, "I said it. I meant it. Something's... wrong with you. Had been with Dani, too."

With that, Jenny marched out of the kitchen and outside. The screen door creaked and then slammed closed once, twice, and on the third finally rested against the frame. Rasa waited, hearing bottles and things shaking in the bin, and the plop of some falling out onto the ground. The grass muffled the stomping steps, and Rasa knew the little girl didn't stop to pick up the ones that fell from the bin.

"Whatever," she muttered in Sasha's voice.

###

Time. A fleeting thing. Sasha Ward, the area's would-be best cosmetologist, was fading after only two years in the field.

Fear. Ever present, nagging, and souring emotion. She tasted it on her tongue. Felt it slither over her skin. It made the grip on the meat tenderizer sweaty.

"What are you?" Jenny asked, with a hard stare at her. Those brown eyes flicking from the edge of the blade in her hand, back to her sister. Sasha. Not Sasha.

Green was the blood of the bog. Green was the blood on the blade. Red was the blood flowing through young Jenny.

"I'm your sister! What has possessed you?!" Her fingertips trailed the green blood from the slash on her back. She pressed the cut cotton to the wound, covering it as best as she could. Deeper, and she would have lost one of her kidneys. The pitifully thin T-shirt did little to help her staunch the flow.

"You're a monster!" Jenny brandished the five-inch blade, circling to place the table between them instead of standing at Sasha's side.

She should have known. The moment Jenny volunteered to help her cut up the venison, she should have denied her. But Sasha wouldn't have. Sasha longed for girl's companionship. Spend time with her family.

"Quiet in there!" their father barked from his permanent residence in the stale recliner.

"Daddy!" Jenny screamed, "Help me!" Her doe eyes were wide, whites showing wildly along the edges. Sweat beaded her brow, and the hand clutching the dripping knife shook.

100

"Hush up!" answered Vic.

Sasha huffed as Rasa's thoughts spilled from her lips. "Useless males."

Jenny deflated, the knife dropping and her hands covering her face. "Why?"

"Why what?"

"Why us?" Jenny cried, throwing her arms wide.

Rasa canted her head, considering for a moment whether to be herself, or to be Sasha. She grinned, Sasha's mouth stretching to fit her own ear to ear smile. "Close to my home. Close to my heart. Easy on the stomach."

Jenny's body shuddered visibly. The girl swallowed, her eyes shifting from the knife on the table to the opening into the living room, before settling on Sasha once more. "Mom?"

"Yes."

"Jer, Kay, and Dani?" The teen choked out, her arms wrapping around her middle, knuckles white with the curl of her fingers around her elbows.

"Yes."

Jenny nodded, her eyes closing, but no tears flowed. "I want... I want to be you."

Rasa laughed, a short bark, before Jenny's eyes met hers. The darkness there. The knowing. She'd witnessed that look before. Once, in a shattered mirror, she had said the same to her creator. "Ask. You have to ask," Rasa's voice rasped, the bog rising in the stolen flesh enveloping her.

Once she made someone, she wouldn't have to skin her meals and take their form. Once she made someone, Jenny's beautifully plain features would forever be hers. Forever young. Forever succulent.

As Jenny, she could evolve. Man-hunter hag. Eating the pubescent boys, and ridding the world of the nasty old men so girls like Jenny could give their lives to more hags. Taste sweeter for her sisters.

"Why do you want this?" She asked, breaking Jenny's wordless nervous shifting and mutterings.

Jenny laughed, her body convulsing with the hyena sounds, "Do you know how many of those bitches in town made fun of me? Mom-less. Sisters dying. My dad being the killer?" Her fists dropped from her elbows and hit the table, the knife clattering. "I can do something with them, right? Like you did with Mom? With Jer and Kay?"

Rasa nodded, smelling the bitter revenge eking from the girl before her. She wondered if revenge would sate Jenny for her long life to come. Rasa knew that loneliness was not cured with becoming a hag. But revenge... that was something to last on.

"And what of me?"

Jenny swallowed, her eyes darting to the knife, then back up to Rasa in her sister's skin, "I can't kill you, can I? I mean... whatever you are... I'd probably die first." Her lips peeled back from her teeth, "While I hate you, I hate them more." She shook her head, "At least Jeridan didn't get beat to death on the daily like Victoria does now. Kaylie woulda ended up in some cult if not for you." Jenny lifted a shoulder, "I've been thinking about you. About us, for a while."

"Obviously." Rasa nodded, not an ounce of sarcasm in her voice, but awe. Her gaze swept toward the living room as the recliner creaked, then settled again. The lazy man probably jerking in his alcoholic sleep. "Revenge."

The teen straightened, nodding, "Revenge." She paused, "Does it have to be all women?"

"No. I prefer females, but we can skin whoever we want." Rasa smiled, and then added, "You must be careful. And meat is your primary source once I give you this life. Understand?"

Jenny's fingers flexed in and out of fists, "I stay in this body until I find another?"

"No, child. I take your body. You get the hag body, and tied to the bog."

"The humpback and everything? The big smile and teeth?"

"You have read too many books," Rasa chided with a snort.

"I couldn't very well ask you everything, now could I?" Jenny retorted.

"I'll teach you. I'll take care of you, like I have for the past eleven years," Rasa soothed, "Ask me."

"How do I word it? I want to be like you. Can you make me like you?" Jenny spread her hands with a lift of her shoulders as she asked.

"Yes. Good enough." Rasa's grin matched her own skin instead of Sasha's as the bog swelled within her and launched toward Jenny out of her mouth and eyes. Green waters, clumps of mud, and chips of bark latched onto Jenny, covering her from the crown of her head to the bottom of her booted feet.

The pristine kitchen glowed a black lit green, shiny on the chrome of the toaster and the steel of stove and oven. Rasa spoke the words her maker spoke, a language before those common today, long lost except to those of the elder magics. The light dried the mound of bog that was once Jenny. Flakes peeled and fell off the girl, floating on the gentle beams to paste themselves on Rasa.

Jenny crumbled. Everything that was her soaked in the bog and transferred to Rasa. She emerged, a new being. Once human, no longer. Hunched and slimed, Jenny's eyes glowed the same green as the magic that took her flesh and gave her new life. She flexed her long, clawed fingers, watching as the four sets of knuckles bent and stretched the pale flesh like a frog breathing in for a croak puffed its skin.

"I feel it." Jenny's voice drowned in the bog made throat. "The magic," she croaked before a wide grin split her pale face and produced rows of black bone jagged teeth.

"Yes." Jenny's voice echoed strong and sure through the room. Rasa moved, the dried bog crumbling away to reveal her new teen body. She stared at what she once was, just as Jenny stared at her. "I will stay here, as you, until you are ready for your own life."

The females grinned at each other. One a beaming, sun-kissed teen, the other a slimy, hunched hag. The bog's waters spread, stretching, growing, always taking.

THE HEART OF THE HAG
KAY PARQUET

Fog blanketed the swamp like a suffocating shroud, clinging to the skeletal trees and stagnant pools. The air reeked of rot, and the water itself pulsed with a sinister life, bubbling as if something below its surface stirred hungrily. A heavy silence hung over the marshlands, broken only by the occasional wet, sucking sound of the muck shifting, as though swallowing something whole.

The swamp was never still. Its magic was ancient, older than time itself; it devoured all who strayed too deep. But more than that, it had a will—a malicious, insatiable hunger that claimed countless souls over the centuries. The swamp and its servant, the Hag, were one.

The marshland was born of blood and betrayal, a cursed place on earth where once there had been teeming life. Long ago, humans tried to harness nature with spells of ancient magic, but failed. Instead, they corrupted life in the swamp and everything around it. Humans came again to tame its wild magics, and the swamp rebelled, turning against them. With its breath of life, it lured the desperate and lost into its clutches. No one left, the swamp taking everything. Their souls, bodies, and screams, swallowed by the muck and darkness.

Many men died here, battles being fought in the past over the centuries the Hag had been alive. They came to the swamps intending to purify the land of its evil influence, and its magic absorbed and twisted them. The waters were replete with their rotting corpses that, to this day, followed the bog's commands. If pitchforks came looking for someone to blame for any death, they would rise to take action.

Women and children perished here as well: the women being changed forever by loss of a child, or a child brought to her after a stillborn death. She couldn't bring them back, but the swamp could.

That gave the swamp a reputation, though, one that wasn't keen on being tested. The Hag herself didn't mess with the swamp and its power. It was its own entity and one who had been here for millennia, way before she was born.

The Hag had long since lost any memory of what it felt like to be human. Her once-beautiful skin now hung in ragged patches from her bones. Clusters of red, pus-filled blisters covered her body, rupturing with every move, emitting a creamy discharge and a smell that rivaled that of the swamp. As quickly as they burst, new sets would replace the old, ready for the perpetual cycle.

There was a time she delighted in still being human and alive, even when infectious rashes painted her skin and the bot flies made their nests in whatever orifice they could find. She had been alive far longer than she cared to remember, and with each passing century, the swamp's grip on her tightened, twisting her deeper into its embrace, deeper into its decay.

But now, the Hag's fingers, gnarled and claw-like, twitched as she moved silently through the mire, her sunken eyes glinting with a feverish hunger.

Beneath the layers of rot and filth, something human still stirred—a buried fragment of the woman she once had been. But that part of her was locked away, smothered beneath the weight of the curse that bound her to this place.

She felt the surface of her present skin, loose and deteriorating, and knew time was of the essence. If she didn't get a new one soon, the swamps' ancient magic would eventually take her. But the skins she used weren't hers; they came from the leftovers of troubled souls who came for help. She and the swamp could bring those with illness or close to death back to vitality, for a price.

Elderly, close to death, pleading for her to cure them, they visited the swamp, thinking the Hag had the answer to save them. She'd give them a chance, a challenge, always mixed with puzzles and rules, knowing they'd never make it. Their defeat nourished the swamp, the darkness swirling in the waters was alive and yearned for its pound of flesh.

Yet, under the Hag's icy shell, hid a profound, unmoving grief. Who she used to be still dwelled in the corners of her mind. Her family had turned on her, blamed her for witchcraft, and thrown her into the swamp to die. They knew it would devour her whole and rid them of her presence, but it didn't. Instead, it took her humanity. Her anger kept her going, but it also left her empty, stuck in a never-ending cycle of revenge and emptiness.

The swamp demanded payment. It always did.

And tonight, it would have its due.

From the depths of the mist, the Hag heard a sound—faint at first, but unmistakable. A desperate cry. She paused, her twisted form melting into the shadows of the trees, her senses sharpening. Someone had come. A new soul, ripe for the taking.

The swamp whispered to her, urging her forward, its dark magic rippling through the brackish water. It craved flesh, life—it craved fear.

A woman stumbled through the fog, clutching a bundled infant to her chest. Her face pale, gaunt, and streaked with sweat and tears. The Hag could sense the sickness radiating from her, the stench of death already clinging to her skin. She watched with cold, gleaming eyes as the woman staggered closer, her breaths coming in labored gasps.

The Hag waded through the bog towards the cry, pieces of her decomposed flesh pulling from her bones with the resistance of the swamp, and stopped before the woman.

She collapsed in the mud before the Hag, her arms shaking, her voice little more than a rasping whisper. "Please... help me... my son... he needs me..."

The Hag remained still, her head tilting ever so slightly as she regarded the stranger. Her cracked lips twisted into a grotesque smile, teeth yellowed and sharp, some missing altogether, like a predator savoring its prey before the kill.

"Help you?" she rasped, her voice as rough as stone. "You come to my swamp, thinking I can save you? Foolish girl. There is always a price."

The young mother's eyes were full of illness, her breath ragged. "I'll do anything... just save him."

The Hag's smile widened, and she leaned in closer, her breath rancid. The woman recoiled, but there was no escape. The swamp held her fast, like a spider drawing in its next meal.

"There is a riddle," the Hag crooned, her voice soft and cold. "Solve it before the next harvest moon, and you will live. Fail..." She left it unspoken.

The woman's lips trembled, and she nodded, her tears mixing with the burbling swamp water.

"I go without legs, I talk without air. I listen without ears, I'm quiet when
dead.

No one touches me, but everyone feels me. What am I?"

The woman's eyes clouded with confusion, her mind already weakened by fear and illness. But she nodded, desperate.

"I will solve it... I swear..."

The Hag leaned over and grinned, a hideous, toothy maw. Thick, brown saliva dripped from a jagged incisor, falling onto the woman's disheveled head. She waved her hand, restoring the woman's strength for the time being.

"The moon is your deadline. Remember that." The woman dragged herself away, clutching her child, her breath still uneven but no longer failing.

For weeks, the Hag watched from the shadows, her eyes glittering with anticipation. The swamp whispered to her, the dark magic swirling in the depths, impatient, wanting to be fed.

The riddle consumed the woman, driving her into madness. She muttered to herself endlessly, her lips cracked and bleeding from the cold, damp air. The young mother no longer tended to her baby, who cried from hunger and neglect. She stared into the murky waters of the swamp from her home where it sat on the bog's edge, her eyes vacant, her mind lost to the words that haunted her.

And when the harvest moon finally rose high above the gnarled trees, she failed.

The woman collapsed into the mud, her heart stuttering to a stop. She had returned to ask for more time, but her body fell limp, eyes open and glassy, staring blankly into the sky. The swamp sighed in satisfaction, and the Hag stepped forward to claim her prize.

The bog felt heavier that night, as if the spirits of those the Hag had tricked were weighing the air down, whispering their bitterness in the fog. She stood over the young woman's body, her hunger faltering.

The skin would be useful—fresh and youthful, not like the wrinkled old corpses she usually harvested. But something about this death gnawed at her. The woman's lifeless eyes, locked open in desperation, reflected her own eternal grief. The part of herself she tried to forget.

She could already feel her own skin, what very little was left of it, slipping from her carcass. If she didn't take the woman's form soon, she'd lose herself completely. She stooped, her fingers tracing the edge of the woman's face, ready to peel the flesh away. Usually she preferred to strip them while they were still alive, delighting with every scream that echoed in the swamps' thick air.

But something else stirred.

The baby's wails cut through the oppressive silence, high-pitched and forlorn, echoing through the fog like a scream from beyond the grave. The Hag paused, her withered hand hovering above the dead woman's skin. She looked toward the child, her eyes narrowing. The baby crawled toward its mother's lifeless body, small hands clawing at the cold, unmoving flesh.

And then, slowly, the baby stopped crying. Its movements stilled. Its eyes—wide, milky, and far too old—turned toward the Hag.

The swamp's magic surged, pouncing, and the child twisted in agony, its limbs elongating, skin paling to a sickly blue-gray. Its face contorted, sharp teeth poking through tiny gums, nails growing into claws. The babe giggled—a sound that should have been innocent, but perverted by the dark magic coursing through its veins.

The Hag recoiled, the swamp's whispers growing louder in her mind. This child was no longer human.

The baby lunged, its tiny body propelled by an unnatural strength, but the Hag swatted it away, her hand shaking as she did so. The child—no, the creature—let out a high-pitched cackle, its mouth splitting open five times its natural size, teeth like knives, pointy and sharp, ready to slice through anyone or anything that stood in its way.

The Hag backed away, what remained of her heart thudded in her chest, the swamp closing in around her like a noose. She turned her gaze back to the woman's body, her skin cold and pale, her face frozen in eternal terror. She should take the skin—finish the ritual, prolong her life for another cycle.

The swamp whispered, but not words of power—instead, laughter, cold and mocking. The Hag felt it tugging at her, the dark magic wrapping around her like chains, pulling her down into the muck. The swamp was playing with her, as it always did, twisting fate and bending it to its cruel, insatiable hunger.

The swamp's dark magic rippled around her. She could feel the power of the curse tightening, threatening to consume her if she strayed too far from her grim duty. But internally, something shifted.

Instead of taking the mother's skin, she gathered the mother with child-creature in tow, taking them deeper into the swamp to a cave she hadn't used in ages. The waters churned as she walked, the swamp purposely resisting her steps, but she pressed on, determined to defy it, if only for this night. She knew she could bring the woman back with a slip of her own life.

The cave was cold and damp, its walls lined with symbols and bones from her long years of dark rituals. She placed her hand over the young woman's chest, feeling the stillness beneath.

The ancient magic surged around her, demanding she complete the ritual and take the skin. But for the first time in ages, she hesitated.

There had to be another way.

Fragments of forbidden spells she swore to forget long ago stirred in her mind. Among them was a spell of life restoration, something far more dangerous and complicated than her usual tricks. It would take some of her own life, and she was ready to give it. There was always a price to pay for magic. Especially when the swamp was involved.

"It will cost me," she thought to herself, "perhaps more than I can pay."

She chanted, her voice low and guttural, drawing on the power of the swamp. The cave trembled around her; the air growing thick with energy. Her hands shook as she carved runes into the woman's skin with one broken, sharp nail, tracing the lines of power pulsing in the earth below them.

The ritual demanded a price, and she felt the swamp's insatiable hunger: it had grown beyond impatience, greedy for the soul it had been promised, even after taking the baby. The Hag grit her teeth and pressed on, pouring every ounce of her remaining magic into the spell.

The Hag's vision blurred. She felt herself slipping, her own life force draining away as the swamp took what it was owed. She could feel her life draining away. She had given too much of herself, though; she did it with little regret thinking she could stop before it sucked her dry.

And yet, she couldn't stop.

With a final, desperate surge, she completed the spell. The woman's breath was shallow but present. The child-creature, sensing his mother's return, wailed.

The Hag could barely stand. Her body, now thin and withered, felt as if made of brittle bone and dust. She gave away too much of herself, far more than she intended.

The swamp howled in fury, its forces tearing at her as she collapsed to the ground. She could feel it consuming her, dragging her back towards the mire, into oblivion.

As the darkness closed in, she smiled. For the first time in centuries, she had done something selfless. The swamp would continue to demand its pound of flesh, but at least in this, mother and child-creature were once more together.

But the bog was not done with its cycle of need.

Within the cave, the woman's body twitched.

Slowly, agonizingly, she stirred. Her limbs moved with a jerky, unnatural motion, like a marionette pulled by invisible strings. The mother's head lolled to the side, her once-lovely face now a mask of death. Her eyes snapped open, glowing with the same sickly light as the child's.

The swamp had claimed her.

The woman rose to her feet, her movements stiff and inhuman. Her lips pulled back in a grotesque smile, her teeth black but her skin still fresh, not sagging and decayed like the Hag's own had been. She let out a low, guttural growl, the sound of something feral and twisted.

The creature that had once been human scuttled to her side, giggling as it clung to its mother's tattered skirts.

A new Hag had been born.

And the swamp sighed, satisfied once more, as its hunger was momentarily sated.

But the cycle would continue.

The swamp always demanded more.

A MURKY RECKONING
C.L. HART

A Horror From the Deep

In his wildest nightmares, the fisherman could never have imagined the horror he dragged aboard his boat from the Gloomwater Sea. He'd heard tales of this monstrosity but had never imagined seeing one. The Abyssal Leviathan spanned nearly ten feet, its oily, swollen body undulating from side to side on the deck of the Nautical Requiem. Its skin was a mottled blend of moldy blues and sickly greens covered in parasitic barnacles.

The creature had a broad, flattened head, a mouth filled with rows of jagged, razor-sharp teeth, and bulbous eyes that reflected a bioluminescent glow, mesmerizing and horrifying. A milky white eye remained stationary, while a brilliant crimson eye darted about, observing its surroundings with suspicion and rage.

Tentacles lined with venomous barbs oozing a noxious glowing chartreuse secretion sprouted from the beast's head. These appendages writhed like snakes preparing to strike. Its serpentine body tapered into a long, whip-like tail covered in spiny protrusions. Sharp ridges ran down its spine along its dorsal edge, pulsing with an eerie blue glow. The creature emitted a miasmal stench of decay and brine. The fisherman covered the beast with a tarpaulin and lashed it to the mast.

An Aquatic Reckoning

Back at the dock, the fisherman hurried to the stables, paying the stable hand four Electrotokens to rent a cart and a pair of mules to haul his catch away. He promised to return the cart and the animals the next day.

Garwick Greedgill was thick around the midsection and had a sunken chest and narrow frame that belied the strength of his wiry arms. His leathery, tanned skin bore witness to many years spent on a boat's deck under the sun's harsh glare. His hair was a bristly mix of silver and gunmetal gray, poking through the many holes in a threadbare red cap embossed with the emblem of a long-forgotten fishing guild. A heavy forehead and scowling brow framed eyes a sickly shade of murky green, reminiscent of a polluted ocean. His broad nose bent slightly to one side courtesy of a mishap with the sail boom. Countless hours spent retrieving catch after catch left his calloused hands stained with fish scales and innards as he searched for the grand haul that always eluded him.

Garwick wore frayed puce trousers held up by a filthy, tattered flaxen rope belt. His once-bright cerise tunic, covered in various colored patches where he had mended it over the years, was threadbare. It hung loosely over his prominent belly. The soles of his scuffed brown boots were worn thin, leaving his feet vulnerable to the cold and damp. He wore a necklace of oddly shaped stones and bones that he believed would attract good luck. The longed-for luck seldom materialized.

Garwick drove the cart as close as possible to the bog extending beyond his property's edge. He lived in a ramshackle hut between the bog and a twisting, moss-covered path that led to a meandering creek. Near the hut was a dingy shed. Every corner held remnants of his profession—a collection of rusty hooks, tattered nets, and an old, cracked barrel filled with miscellaneous items of dubious worth. A box containing lucky tokens collected over the years sat on a dusty shelf. Best of all, there was a wondrous grimoire. An odor of decay emanated from the book's brown hide cover. Garwick did not mind the strange texture or unpleasant scent of the tome. Based on today's catch, the grimoire's magic had already begun to work.

The Fortune Teller's Gift

Garwick recalled the night he received the book. As he was drinking away his troubles in Gromnar Goldfin's Tavern, he was approached by Finnegan Scaleweaver, an old druid who earned his living by telling fortunes to the local farmers and fishermen.

Garwick was barely a man when he started working for Finnegan's older brother Galileo. The young fisherman's skills impressed Galileo so much that he took him on as a business partner. It all started well, but then the business hit a rough patch. Both men began drinking heavily. A dispute broke out one evening on the deck of the Nautical Requiem over allegations of shortfalls in the coffers. The pair fought, tumbling from the deck into the Gloomwater Sea. A combination of resentment and potent spirits fueled Garwick's fury. Overpowering Galileo, he held him underwater. It was too late when Garwick finally relented and pulled Galileo to shore.

Finnegan did not demand Garwick's arrest or any part of the business except a ten percent share of the profits. Garwick considered this a reasonable resolution. He almost felt guilty, realizing he did not deserve such kindness.

Finnegan stood before Garwick, smiling like a child who has made a remarkable discovery.

"'Tis good to see you, old lad, but I would be remiss if I failed to tell you that you reek of rotting fish," Garwick said. "I only mention this because it may drive away your customers. Nobody wants his fortune told by a man with such a vile stench about him."

"It is not I who reeks of rotting fish; it is the grimoire I have in my bag," Finnegan explained as he sat down. "It is a gift for you."

"You are the mystic, not me," Garwick said, wondering if Finnegan was losing what remained of his senses. "What would I need this book for?"

"Because I wrote the spells in the book for you," Finnegan said. "If you follow the steps outlined in this grimoire, your luck will change. You will break the curse preventing you from succeeding."

"Which would benefit you as well," Garwick noted.

"Of course, but what's wrong with that? Your focused mind is the reason my brother selected you and not me as his business partner."

"I have always wondered, Finnegan, did you resent your brother's choice?"

"Not at all. I approved of his decision. Business bores me, and I would not wish to be at sea all day. Go on, open the book! You will see that I have outlined ceremonies in an easy-to-follow fashion, complete with chants to summon the Bog Hag."

"The old sorceress said to dwell at the center of the swamp? I certainly don't believe such nonsense. It's the sort of tale told to scare children so they don't drown their fool selves searching for treasure in the bog. Are you saying the witch is real?"

"Oh, aye, and I've even given you her name so you can address her correctly when you perform your spell."

"Yadira of the Roots, daughter of Nyarlathotep the Wish-Bringer," Garwick read. He sighed, giving the fortune teller a sideways glance as he sipped a golden fruit drink heavy on the rum. He signaled the waiter.

"Lee, another for me and one for my fanciful friend," he said.

"This first spell is the essence of simplicity," Garwick noted. "All that is required is a bowlful of swamp water, a bit of my blood, a handful of muck, and one of my treasures. There isn't even an animal sacrifice required, only three raven feathers."

"You neglected to mention the most important component of the spell," the fortune teller noted. "You must state your intent with your voice and your full heart. Your desire must be so much a part of you that it carries on your blood. When she senses the power of your conviction, Yadira will accept your sacrifice and send her message to you in dreams. I have all the tools you need here in this satchel. There are potions and powders, a dagger, a willow circle, a ceremonial candle, a raven's feathers, and a scrying bowl. Begin tonight, and tomorrow, you will be blessed."

When Garwick returned home that night, he considered going to bed and forgetting the strange, smelly book with its peculiar spells, but he was drunk enough to hope there was magic left in the world. He retrieved the items from the bag given to him by Finnegan Scaleweaver - a scrying bowl made of yellow stone and a ceremonial dagger with an awe-inspiring muted red handle and a wavy greenish-black blade. After assembling the items he required for the first spell, he took them to the banks of the bog in an old fishing basket made of gray-gold beach grass. He lit a fire in a pit as he chanted, throwing a handful of acrid yellow powder into the flames. Then he lit a lantern to read the instructions for the spell.

An Incantation To Summon Yadira of the Roots, Daughter of Nyarlathotep the Wish-Bringer

Ingredients:

- A handful of muck from the bog

- Three feathers from a raven or crow

- A stone bowl filled with murky water

- A sprig of willow bent into a circular arc

- A candle made from beeswax or tallow, shaped like a gnarled tree

- A sacrament of sacrifice

Preparation:

1. **Build the Altar:** Arrange the items in a circular formation. Place the scrying bowl at the center.

2. **Anoint Thyself:** Using the swamp water, anoint your forehead, heart, and palms. Declare now, "In water, in earth, in air, and in shadow, I call forth the Ancient Powers."

3. **Create the Circle:** Make a cut sufficient to draw adequate blood to anoint the willow sprig. Take the sprig and lay it in a circle around the bowl. This circle serves as the threshold between realms.

4. **Light the Candle:** Anoint your candle with blood. As you light the candle, declare: "By wax and wick, I beckon thy presence, Yadira, guardian of roots and murky truths."

The Incantation:

Drain a few drops of blood into the stone bowl. Add to this the Potion of Summoning and the Dust of Time. With your hands over the bowl, gaze into its depths while speaking the ancient words:

"From depths of mire, from shadows cast,

I summon thee, daughter of future and past.

Rooted stalks and decaying leaves,

Like your lost mother, mortal fates do you weave.

Lurker in mist, mother of the bog;

Throw off now the shroud of fog.

By raven's feather and willow's grace,

Guide my spirit to your place."_

5. **Offerings:** Scoop a handful of muck into the bowl, forming a small mound. Press your sacrifice into the muck and place the feathers atop it.

6. **Wait for the Response:** Sit in repose for several minutes, contemplating your wish. If Yadira accepts your sacrifice, she shall make

her presence known through visions, whispers, or the rustling of leaves.

Closing the Ritual:

When you sense your time of communion has ended, thank Yadira for her presence, extinguish the candle, and dismantle the circle. Pour the contents of the bowl into the bog and drop the willow circle in after them, closing the door between realms.

If the summoning is successful and Yadira appears in person or in a dream, speak to her with reverence, or you may only live long enough to regret your error. State your purpose clearly and respectfully. Should the witch grant you her wisdom or aid, present her with an offering from your heart—a token of gratitude and respect.

Warning:

Tread carefully; Yadira's nature is as wild and ancient as the bog she inhabits. Like her father, she does not grant requests lightly, and her wisdom comes at a price. Approach with humility and respect her power.

"It was kind of Scaleweaver to include the items I need to perform this spell," Garwick said. "If this summoning is successful, I'll ask the witch to bless the old fellow for his generosity."

Garwick felt giddy as he began.

"If this works, it will be worth the sacrifice of my Four-Lobed Luminara medallion," he said, pressing the item into the muck. "It pains me to lose it as it was a gift from my old partner Galileo, bestowed on me forty years ago. Ah, well, I'm sure he'd understand. Our business is well nigh on its deathbed. If I don't find plentiful bounty soon, I may have to become a farmer. Perish the thought! Please don't let that be my fate,

Daughter of Nyarlathotep."

With the spell at its end, Garwick sat in repose, feeling more alive and at peace than he ever had. Suddenly, a breeze blew out the candle.

"Rest now, Garwick Greedgill," a chill voice whispered in the wind. "I have heard your call. It is time to walk through the door into the world beyond the wall of sleep."

Garwick's Dream

That night, Garwick dreamed he was aboard the Nautical Requiem. The small, waterlogged form of a young drowned woman lay on the ship's deck, her skirts pushed up as Garwick defiled her body. The skies were dark, and the sea was stormy. A lone candle shaped like a tree burned on the ship's prow.

Garwick gazed into the flickering candle flame as yellow and orange tendrils danced and twisted like waves. The candle's light illuminated the lines of time etched on his face. The impossibly robust flame pulsed as if heralding something from beyond the known world. A figure cloaked in seaweed and shadows emerged from the flame, her long hair flowing like strands of kelp swaying in the current. Her face was at once beautiful and terrifying. Her glowing crimson eyes gleamed like polished stones pulled from the seabed, revealing wisdom, sorrow, and ancient hunger.

"You are more comely than I expected, Yadira of the Roots," Garwick greeted, pulling up his trousers and lowering the drowned woman's skirts. "I expected you to be a crone, but you are a strangely lovely woman in her prime. Please accept my apologies for what you have just witnessed. It has been many years since I lay with a woman, and...

well, after all, she's not apt to complain, is she?"

The apparition's lips spread into an impossibly wide grin, revealing sharp teeth and curved fangs. The strands of her hair undulated on the nocturnal wind like snakes. As she raised her hand, the corpses of fishermen long lost at sea rose from the depths.

"Turn away if you do not wish theirs to become your fate," the creature tittered. "However, should you do so, you will miss out on the bounty that waits in the depths of the abyss."

Garwick awoke with a start. At the moment, the life of a farmer seemed very attractive. As his feet touched the floor, his mood changed.

"The witch is testing me," he surmised. "No hideous night vision will scare Garwick Greedgill from his quest for glory. I respect your game, Yadira of the Roots. You'll not let me have my wish easy as that. However, I've been married to the sea since I was a lad. She can be a harsh bitch, but also a generous mistress. I feel you're much the same, and I intend to reward you handsomely for your gifts."

Bogs, Hags, and Things Brought In On the Tide

When he stepped outside that morning to head to the docks, Garwick heard faint whispers from the bog. As he stood beside the rented cart now, watching the captive aquatic horror writhe within the confines of the tarpaulin, he heard them again. He believed mystic forces had sent the Abyssal Leviathan to him to use as a sacrifice.

Garwick dragged the Leviathan out of the cart. It hit the ground with an oily plop, emitting a gurgling snarl. He lashed the beast to a tree near the bog and moved the cart closer to his hut. He did not wish to pay for a destroyed cart or mules eaten by the thrashing monstrosity from the depths.

Garwick went to the bathhouse and stoked a fire on a metal plate. He slid the plate beneath a platform upon which a porcelain tub sat. Hurrying to his house, he fetched the foul-smelling grimoire, his fishing basket filled with potions and powders, his golden stone scrying bowl, and his ceremonial dagger. He returned to the spot where the Leviathan writhed and snarled in its bonds. A manic gleam illuminated his eyes as he unwrapped the tarpaulin from the beast's torso. He left its upper and lower portions covered so it could not bite him with its fang-filled mouth, strike him with its toxic tentacles, or hit him with its barbed tail.

Garwick slathered the Leviathan's torso with a paste made from swamp muck mixed with the liquid in the bowl. His chanting rose in pitch and volume as he raised his dagger, plunging it into the beast's thick hide. The dagger snapped from its hilt as he attempted to draw it down the Leviathan's body. Moving surprisingly quickly for a man with such a stout build, he hurried to his supply hut, where he retrieved a boat hook. After smearing the boat hook with swamp paste, he forced it into the notch created by the dagger. He dragged the hook downward with all his strength.

The beast's innards spilled out in a wretched, stinking stew, killing the surrounding foliage. Garwick leaped back, scuffing his boots against the unsullied ground. Corrosive blood pitted the soles but, fortunately, did not reach Garwick's feet.

When the Leviathan finally stopped moving, Garwick tentatively approached it, poking it with the boat hook. He dragged the dead creature to the bog using the tarpaulin and rolled it into the water, taking care not to come into contact with its corrosive blood.

"Yadira of the Roots, accept my sacrifice!" Garwick called in a resonant voice. "In return, I ask you to hear my plea. I wish to be the most renowned fisherman in the kingdom and have future generations tell tales of my adventures."

A Fateful Encounter

Garwick stripped off his stinking clothes and left them outside the bath hut. He climbed into the tub and found the water at an optimal temperature, which he interpreted as a positive sign. Despite his fifty-seven-year-old body protesting that he should stay home and rest after his eventful day, Garwick's spirit was filled with the desire to celebrate his triumph at Goldfin's Tavern. He was blissfully unaware of the Abyssal Leviathan poking its head above the surface of the bog, then swimming off, making noises that sounded not unlike mirthful chuckles.

After finishing his bath, Garwick put on a pair of slippers, wrapped himself in a towel, and strolled to his hut. He selected a shamrock green tunic with russet trousers and a newish pair of grullo suede shoes. He slicked his thinning hair with spice-scented pomade and trimmed his scruffy beard. Taking his favorite money purse made from sturdy, light red cloth, he left for Goldfin's.

The patrons at Goldfin's greeted Garwick civilly, but he couldn't count any among them as his friends. His grumpy demeanor and tendency toward backstabbing ensured he had none of those. He ordered a pitcher full of brassy-colored brew and tossed a bag containing seven Whitegreens to Goldfin in a gesture of goodwill.

Garwick found an empty table in the corner. He sat down and

sipped his drink, watching the other patrons gossip, play darts, or dance. A strange man approached his table.

The newcomer shone like a freshly minted Greenstrike. His bearing was regal, and he was undeniably handsome with his dusky complexion and black hair flowing over his shoulders like a cascading waterfall. His canny eyes were the color of darkest night. He wore a silken suit the same shade as a rain-wet minthaleaf. A wide-brimmed hat sat rakishly atop his glorious head. He tipped his hat, gracing Garwick with a crooked smile.

"May I join you, sir?" the stranger inquired.

"As you wish, but you'll pay for your own," Garwick started. Recalling his recent good fortune, he changed his approach. He signaled the waiter.

"Another mug for my friend, if you would, my fine fellow," he said, crossing the young man's palm with a bag containing five Whitegreens.

The lad hurried off, returning quickly with a mug.

"Will you be dining this evening, Mr. Garwick?" the waiter asked.

"You know, I'd almost forgotten me stomach," Garwick laughed. "There's something about being surrounded by the smell of fish all day that wreaks havoc on the appetite. Yes, me bucko, we'll dine. Goldfin makes a fine stew of fowl with vegetables topped by dumplings. Will you join me for a bowl, sir?"

"I will. That certainly sounds like a treat after my long journey.

Thank you kindly," the newcomer said, extending his hand. "Greystoke Gleamscale at your service."

"Garwick Thistlebloom Greedgill," Garwick said. "I've not seen you in these parts before, Mr. Gleamscale. Or is it Count, Duke, or Lord Gleamscale? You certainly have a noble demeanor."

"I hail from far beyond this realm," Gleamscale replied. "However, I have my connections. You are hoping to contact she who is known as Yadira of the Roots. I am here to help you facilitate that contact."

"I am grateful for aid from the emissary of the storied Bog Hag," Garwick said. "Does she have a preferred title, perhaps high priestess or mage?"

"Madam Yadira will do," Gleamscale said. "Now, let us get down to business. I have a gift for you, but first, I'll have you draw a card."

Gleamscale reached into a green canvas carrying bag decorated with a picture of a black cat with oversized white eyes. Gleamscale drew a deck of Tarot cards from the bag.

"I see your cat carries a fish with gleaming silver scales in its mouth," Garwick noted. "Is this image your calling card, or do you simply appreciate its aesthetic qualities?"

"The bag was a gift from a friend. My daughter gave this deck of cards to me."

Gleamscale shuffled the cards eight times, asked Garwick to cut the deck, and then shuffled it five more times, asking Garwick to take the top card.

The card depicted a sailor standing on a dock overlooking a stormy sea. Five men dressed in uniforms of the royal guard stood on the deck of a ship, each armed with a sword. The choppy water looked like it was moving, and the guardsmen appeared quite alive. A westerly wind lifted the sailor's thin hair.

"Five of Swords," Gleamscale noted. "Stormy seas lie ahead, but the battle is not yet won or lost. There is still time to turn back."

"I'll not be turning back, Master Gleamscale," Garwick assured his companion as the waiter set two bowls of stew before the pair. "I'm going to stay the course. I don't mean to brag, but I caught an Abyssal Leviathan this afternoon! I sacrificed this beast to the bog. Do you suppose Madam Yadira has noticed my efforts?"

Gleamscale confirmed, "We have noted your sacrifice. I did not take you for one to turn back from a challenge. This gift will help further your efforts. Have it with my blessing, but take care that in your enthusiasm, you do not ignore the signs."

Gleamscale handed Garwick a glorious grimoire. Despite its captivating rose ebony cover, the book was unsettling. It smelled like dead flowers in a mausoleum.

"Mr. Gleamscale, this is an incredible gift," Garwick exclaimed. "I thank you, good sir. I only ask if you possibly have something in which I may wrap this fine tome. I would hate to think of it being exposed to the elements were it to rain or to have it stolen by some covetous sort envying my good fortune."

"I have something even better than a cloth," Gleamscale replied. "What say you to a new carrying bag with a fresh dagger to replace the one that broke off in the belly of the Abyssal Leviathan, as well as an extra supply of potions and powders?"

"I would say you are too kind, good emissary," Garwick said, his eyes alight like a child receiving a special gift for his birthday celebration. "Alas, the hour grows late, and I must take my leave if I am to stand a chance of rising at an optimal hour to begin my hunt for fish worth selling. The poison seas are so depleted that I fear I must ply my trade elsewhere. I am long in the tooth to consider a move, yet a retirement in the golden land would be a balm for my soul. Do you have a place to stay tonight, Mr. Gleamscale? I haven't much to offer, but if you are in need..."

"I must attend to duties elsewhere, but I am honored to walk you home," Gleamscale offered.

"I am happy for your company. Ruffians troll these roads, hoping to rob an honest man of his hard-earned gain. Despite your fine attire, I sense these highwaymen would not trouble you. You have an air of power about you if I might be so bold as to say."

"You carry yourself in the manner of a man not to be trifled with as well," Gleamscale noted.

"I'll use my new knife to gut any troublemaker who messes with us," Garwick smirked. "I thank you again for these fine gifts. They were quite an unexpected delight."

"Think nothing of it, my good fellow. I enjoy granting wishes. You will find Madam Yadira equally generous if you approach her respectfully."

"I'd have it no other way," Garwick promised. "A venerable lady of such power deserves the highest regard."

A Night Fraught With Peril

"Those blasted herons sound like tortured souls wailing in the bowels of hell," Garwick complained as he and Gleamscale walked along the misty path to his home. "I'd rustle one up for tomorrow's dinner with my bow, but they aren't good eating. They're poison, just like everything else in this area. Do you know, some days I consider giving up fishing to raise fowl? 'Tis practically the only meat I care to eat anymore."

"Raising fowl sounds like a fine idea," Gleamscale agreed. "Perhaps you should seriously consider it."

"Alas, I would miss the sea too much," Garwick said wistfully. "She has been my only mistress. She is a demanding wench, but on the occasions when she shows me her generosity, it is well worth it. 'Tis a pity that these days she only has mutated horrors to offer. Well-a-day, here we are. I know you've mysterious things to be about, but the invitation to rest here remains open. I would allow you my bed while I sleep on a cot."

"There is goodness in your heart, sir. If you pay it heed, it will see you through to better things. And now, I bid you good night. Use your new gifts wisely."

Gleamscale strode away into the mists.

"What is he?" Garwick wondered aloud as he unlocked his front door. "He's of noble bearing but not soft like most nobles. He walks about wearing silken suits, carrying no weapons that I could see, yet any man who attempted to waylay him would be a damn fool."

Garwick lit a lantern and cleared a space on his cluttered dining table. He emptied the sturdy, rufous carrying bag onto its surface.

"Look at these fine things!" Garwick marveled. "My sacrifice must have pleased the old hag for her to send her emissary to give me such a present."

Garwick opened the grimoire. The language was like none he'd ever seen. Disappointment filled him, but he inhaled the fine blue dust covering the pages when he breathed in. He sneezed, and the letters rearranged themselves in a manner he could understand.

"A Spell for Oneiromancy," he read aloud. "The Dreamer shall drink a draught of Potion of the Enchanted Wood. Why, that must be this one. It's green like trees. Its label even confirms it to be so. Next, the spell says to chew on the Golden Berry of Moonlit Knowledge and advises me to heed what I learn behind the walls of sleep. May this spell help me locate my next sacrifice for Madam Yadira of the Roots."

Garwick drank the dream elixir.

"This is divine!" he declared. "It tastes like the delicious pastries made by the old baker I worked for as a youth."

He popped a golden berry into his mouth and bit down.

"This tastes like the blood-red berries on the Whisperbloom bush," he realized. "A bit tart but delicious. Madam Yadira must appreciate my efforts to reward me with such a delightful treat. Now I am off to the Land of Slumber, where I hope to learn what action to take next."

Garwick climbed onto his lumpy old mattress. His worn red blanket smelled of fish. It pleased him that the well-heeled Gleamscale had declined his offer of accommodation. Providing such a bed for a distinguished gentleman would have been embarrassing.

"I wonder if Gleamscale needs to sleep," Garwick mused. "Perhaps he spends nights flapping over the bog like a faceless bat."

A Call to Sacrifice

Garwick heard a beautiful female voice singing. To his surprise, he realized the sound was coming from the bog. He strode from his hut to the bog's edge as if walking on air.

"Come and show yourself, my lovely," he invited. "I desire with all my heart to see the one singing so fine a song."

What rose from the bog was both hideous and seductive. Her body was ideally proportioned, with pert, firm breasts. Her skin was the same color and texture as the Abyssal Leviathan's. Luminous locks of hair the color of swamp muck fell over her shoulders. A thatch of hair in the same hue covered her pubic mound. The swamp siren motioned for Garwick to approach.

"Come, Garwick, you can't deny you're intrigued," she teased. "After all, you've not been with a woman, not even a whore, in twenty years. Well, not a living woman anyway."

"What price would I have to pay to sample your wares, she-devil?" Garwick wondered.

"That's for you to decide," the mocking seductress smirked. "In the meantime, why not let the moon's whispers guide you? It's only you and me here. You are a grown man with no ties to wife or sweetheart, are you not?"

"Yes, and you are—what are you, madam? Are you a nightmare manifested in my mind by that potion given to me by the emissary of the Bog Witch? Are you a demon? Or are you the ghost of the monster I sacrificed, hoping to exact your revenge by preying on a man's desires for female company? Your coloring, after all, is the same moldy, corrupted hue as its hide!"

Garwick gripped the siren's wrist. She laughed as he pulled her towards him. As he viewed her at close range, he recoiled in horror. The siren's lustrous locks were writhing serpents. Her eyes were empty sockets with aquatic worms feasting on the remaining bits of flesh. With a snarl, she exposed sharp, curved fangs resembling those of a viper.

"What manner of fiend are you?" he demanded.

"What's the matter, Garwick? Don't you want me?" the siren goaded. "I didn't take you for the fussy sort. I have it on good authority that you once stuck your pole into the mayor's poor drowned daughter after you fished her up from the water. Once you'd finished defiling the poor young lady's corpse, you made yourself out to be a hero, reporting your grim find to the harbor patrol, your normally boisterous voice subdued by mock sorrow."

The enraged fisherman lunged at the mocking siren. She made no struggle against him, her incessant tittering driving him to the brink of madness as he wrapped his hands around her throat and squeezed.

A Waking Nightmare

As a chill breeze swept over Garwick, he awoke with a start. His feet were wet and cold. He jumped when he felt a hand grip his arm. He made a squawking sound similar to the cry of a startled nightbird as he gazed into the face of Finnegan Scaleweaver.

"What are you doing lurking around my yard with that black hood pulled over your head like a reaper?" Garwick demanded. "Were you planning to rob me?"

"Not at all," Scaleweaver replied. "It's a fortunate thing I was passing by, don't you suppose? You were about to fall into the bog."

"I find it interesting that you decided to lurk around my home on this night of all nights," Garwick retorted. "You've been setting me up, haven't you?"

"Friend fisherman, your terrible dream unsettles you," Scaleweaver soothed. "Let us hasten to your home, and I'll brew you a cup of tea to calm your nerves."

"Yes, I suppose it couldn't hurt," Garwick agreed. "I wonder what made me come out here. I'm not prone to sleepwalking."

"Perhaps it was moon madness inspiring your midnight stroll," the druid suggested. "The moon is in her full glory tonight."

"Yes, and I drank the potion and ate the berry given to me by the emissary of Yadira of the Roots," Garwick revealed. "Have you seen him, Finnegan? He is marvelous to behold! At first, he looks the part of a delicate nobleman with his sleek black hair flowing down his back and his fancy clothes. However, when you see the set of his jaw and the flint in his midnight eyes, you know he is not one to be trifled with. I am sure he knows magic that I, or even you, with your knowledge of deities and spirits, cannot imagine. If I could learn his secrets, I would forego this ridiculous life of trawling for the big haul with nothing to show for it."

"The life of a mystic is not for the faint of heart," Scaleweaver advised as the pair entered Garwick's hut.

"Nor is the life of a fisherman," Garwick countered.

"That is true," Scaleweaver agreed. He strolled to the fireplace and stoked the flames, adding another log. He hung the kettle over the fire.

"Will you show me the gifts the emissary gave you while we wait for the water to boil?" Scaleweaver wondered.

"Why not?" Garwick agreed. "Look upon them while I tell my tale. I performed the Ceremony of Revelation in the tome you gave me. On the first night, I heard whispers from the bog and had a terrifying dream that almost prompted me to abandon my quest. However, I persisted, and yesterday afternoon, I hauled an Abyssal Leviathan onto my boat."

"Truly? I thought the Abyssal Leviathan was the stuff of legend."

"It is clear that at least one of the beasts existed. I took this find as a blessing. I sacrificed the creature to the bog. The Bog Hag's emissary appeared at Goldfin's Tavern that evening, and he gave me this fine bag containing these wonderful items. As you can see, the grimoire is written in a strange tongue. At first, I was deeply disappointed. However, I breathed in the fine blue dust covering the pages, and suddenly, I could read the script. I followed the instructions for the first spell, but thus far, the only thing to come of it was a dream of a she-fiend who rose from the bog to taunt me."

"A she-fiend?" Scaleweaver inquired, looking curiously at his companion.

"Yes. I suppose the dream resulted from drinking the intoxicating potion that tasted like the wonderful pastries I enjoyed during childhood. The body of this horror was the finest female form, but it was covered in the same oily, corrupt hide as the body of the Abyssal Leviathan. Furthermore, her head was covered in writhing serpents, and her black-lipped mouth contained the fangs of a serpent."

"This sounds like a dreadful vision indeed," Scaleweaver commiserated. "Ah, the kettle sings! Let us pour the water and allow our tea to steep."

Garwick watched as Scaleweaver spooned tea leaves into the hot water.

"Let us see what the next spell in your glorious grimoire advises. Well, isn't that fortuitous? It's a divining spell. That should be a simple matter with your wonderful scrying bowl."

"You can read this language?" Garwick inquired.

"Of course I can. Known it all my life, I have. But you didn't need me to read it, did you? The gods provided you with what you needed. Fetch me the scrying bowl, friend fisherman, and your fate will become clear."

Garwick brought the stone bowl to Scaleweaver. He followed the druid outside, eyeing him suspiciously.

"You aren't so addled as you pretend, are you, Fortune Teller?" he asked.

"I pretend at nothing, sir," Scaleweaver insisted. "Sometimes, the thoughts swirl about my head at such a rate that I might appear dizzy, but I'm simply pondering. Now, it's off to the bog with us to gather water in the bowl. Bring a lantern, won't you? We'll need a light by which to see the visions."

"I can't put my finger on it, but something is different about you tonight."

"Well, aren't we all different from one day to the next? Come, come, let us determine your next course of action."

"My next action is to demand what trick you are playing on me. There is no Bog Hag, is there?"

"There most assuredly is. As I told you, she is the daughter of the Wish Bringer from beyond the stars!"

"You claimed she demands a sacrifice. I sacrificed a mighty creature to her today, yet all this brought me was horrible dreams of a swamp demon attempting to seduce me, dredging terrible memories from the muck of my subconscious."

"Calm yourself, friend fisherman. Allow me to extract just a few drops of blood from your person to mix with the bog water so that we may look into your future."

"You'll not murder me and take what money I have remaining, Grifter!" Garwick bellowed.

Murder Most Murky

The expression on Scaleweaver's face was one of baffled surprise as Garwick charged forward, thrusting his new dagger into the fortune teller's heart. Scaleweaver gave a low moan and crumpled to the ground. Garwick kicked the dying man in the ribs.

"I don't know if you and that dandy were conspiring to steal my fortune, but I've gotten rid of you at least," Garwick bragged. "The moon is still in full, glorious bloom, and you are my next sacrifice to the Bog Hag. If I can find the pretty fellow, I'll gladly add him to the roster. Should he fail to turn up, I suppose those mangy mules must do."

Garwick slit Scaleweaver's throat and rolled his body into the bog.

"Yadira of the Roots!" he called, his quivering voice punctuated by episodes of maniacal laughter. "Accept my sacrifice and grant me my wish! I shall be the most renowned fisherman in the realm, and each generation will tell tales of my exploits. If you need another sacrifice from me, send me your emissary so that I may thrust my blade into his heart and spill his pristine blood into this polluted bog!"

"Well, there's a simple wish to grant. Here I am, my good fellow. Stab away if it will make you feel better."

The wondrous Greystoke Gleamscale strode out of the shadows and stood before Garwick, holding his arms wide.

"Where in all the hells did you come from?" Garwick demanded.

"Me? I was flapping around over the swamp like a faceless bat," Gleamscale replied. "Well, come on. Stab me like you did old Scaleweaver. Drown me like you did his brother Galileo forty years ago."

"It was me or him!" Garwick insisted. "He would have ruined me!"

"So you say," Gleamscale said with a shrug. "Well, are you going to sacrifice me, man? Go on, stab me through the heart. Gouge out my eyes. Slit my throat. Do whatever you wish. I'm here at your pleasure."

What remained of Garwick Greedgill's rationale begged him to drop the knife and run, but his hot temper won the day. He rammed the dagger into the breast of the glorious being, whom he was by now sure was not a man. Tarry black blood ran from the wound, staining Gleamscale's spotless shirt.

Gleamscale staggered back, his expression one of horrified surprise, as if he had not expected Garwick to go through with his threat. Then he stood straight up, laughed, and waved his hand over the wound. It disappeared, and his shirt also returned to its previous pristine condition. Gleamscale opened his arms.

"Won't you join me, my dears?" he invited. "I think it's time we showed Mr. Greedgill the truth."

As Garwick gaped in horror, Finnegan Scaleweaver's corpse rose from the bog, accompanied by the putrescent siren. Scaleweaver opened his arms, shook his head, and assumed the form of a silver-haired, ancient, yet powerful crone. Garwick noticed she had the same black eyes as the magnificent Gleamscale, the same dusky complexion, and a similar quirking grin.

"He is your son?" Garwick asked the witch, pointing a trembling finger toward Gleamscale.

"My father," the crone replied.

"And you are..."

"Your people call me Yadira of the Roots. My sire is Nyarlathotep the Wish-Bringer. My mother is Nathicana, Weaver of

Destiny, queen of the lost world of Zaïs."

"Is this creature your pet?" Garwick wondered, his lip curling in disgust as he gestured toward the siren.

"That is a very ungentlemanly assessment, sir," Nyarlathotep-Gleamscale chided. "This is Mormo, the Thousand-Faced Moon, a dear friend to my daughter and me. Mr. Greedgill finds your current form unsettling, Mormo. Would you consider altering it?"

"I think not," Mormo replied. "I like it. However, I can assure Mr. Greedgill that my unseemly appearance will not trouble him much longer."

"You know, Mr. Greedgill, my daughter and I can take food or leave it," Nyarlathotep noted. "Mormo, however, has a very hearty appetite. If she doesn't feed regularly, she becomes out of sorts."

"It isn't pleasant when I'm out of sorts," Mormo giggled. "I wreak terrible havoc when I neglect my appetite. You would be honored to help me regain my equilibrium, wouldn't you, Mr. Greedgill?"

"No!" Garwick protested, backing away. He stumbled over a branch, landing on his backside. The horror from the bog approached him with a scintillating stride. Her forked tongue flicked out to slick hungrily over her lips. Her powerful hands drew her victim to her, her fangs piercing his throat as the greedy mouths of the snakes writhing on her head latched onto his flesh.

The last thing Garwick Greedgill saw as his consciousness faded was the real Finnegan Scaleweaver stepping from behind the trees. He knelt before Nyarlathotep and Yadira, kissing the backs of their hands.

"I have avenged my brother and poor Marcela Jardine," the druid said. "Galileo came to me in a dream the night after his passing, advising me not to seek revenge on Greedgill. However, as you know, I was out for a sail on the day Greedgill found Marcela's body. When I saw him defiling her corporeal vessel, the need for revenge rose in me along with disgust. She was a sweet, delicate young woman, often sickly but always brimful of encouragement for others. I am forever grateful to the three of you for answering my call. Name your price, and I will make good on my bargain."

"While the bog is resilient, pollution overwhelms the seas," Yadira noted. "There are brave fishermen ready to stand against greedy company owners who contaminate the waters. You may repay your debt to us by making it your mission to assist them."

"Success is yours with the resources we leave for you," Nyarlathotep assured. "Your brother is proud of you, Finnegan. He will tell you so himself when you meet him behind the walls of sleep."

Acknowledgments

Nyarlathotep is the creation of H. P. Lovecraft. He initially appears in a story of the same name, first published in the November 1920 issue of *The United Amateur*.

Mormo is the creation of H. P. Lovecraft. She appears in *The Horror At Red Hook*, first published in the January 1927 issue of *Weird Tales*.

Nathicana and Zaïs are the creations of H. P. Lovecraft. They appear in the poem *Nathicana*, first published in the Spring 1927 issue of *The Vagrant*.

All other characters are the original creations of this author. Yadira appears in several stories in my *Tales From the Dreamlands* series. In this story, she almost ends up being a MacGuffin, allowing her BFF, her father, and Garwick Greedgill's obsessions to do the heavy lifting. However, she adds an enjoyable element of surprise—enjoyable if you're not Garwick Greedgill, that is.

Missing

Kyle Thomas

"Today is the thirteenth anniversary of a 12-year-old from the neighboring town who went for a walk and never returned," Jimmy said to Tim as they sat at a table. "The local paper has an article about all the people who went missing over the last 20 years."

"Sucks for that kid's family," Tim said as he put $15 down to pay the tab, "to have a reminder every year that your son is missing. Hard to get any closure."

"Yeah, who knows what weirdo is out there snatching little kids up. I bet the kid didn't carry his dad's 45 caliber pistol with him. That would do some damage to a person trying to pick off a kid," Jimmy said, patting his belly and remembering the delicious pile of bacon and eggs he just ate. "Bears don't like .45s, either."

Tim motioned to Jimmy's thigh holster. "I don't understand why you brought that thing. It's not like we're going to come across a grizzly or mountain lion. There are no man eaters in the Appalachians.

Only snakes, bears, and leeches. Snakes bite, bears eat your food, and leeches stick their tongue in you and suck your blood."

"Whatever man," Jimmy tapped the article's headline, 'Missing'. "People disappear around here and I ain't taking any chances."

Your ankle feel any better?" He asked, looking at the swollen lump and darkened skin just above Tim's left sock. "That was a hell of a tweak yesterday. It's a good thing it's only sprained and not broken."

"Yeah, but I'd like to hang here one more day just to make sure I'm healed enough. Slamming my foot between that boulder and tree root is not something I want to take lightly. We only have fifty-three more miles to go and six days to do it. We got time."

"I'd like to spend that extra time in the hotel bar picking up chicks," Jimmy stated as he winked at the cute redhead waitress who took Tim's money. "Tell you what, I'll hike to the next site, set things up, and wait for you."

"Dude, it's almost eleven. You won't make it to the site until after dark and it looks like you've spotted a chick already. Wait till tomorrow, man. Don't be stupid," Tim said.

"I'm not going to treat a lady to my masculine wiles smelling like corn chips and old gym socks. Besides, I don't want to ask if she can bring a friend for my lame hiking buddy. Maybe we should stick a leech on you to reduce the swelling."

"It's weird your mom named you after a little dick when you're such a big one," Tim retorted while flipping the bird.

"She named me James, I chose Jimmy. It's like calling a big guy Tiny," Jimmy said as he stood, nearly bumping into the back of a brunette waitress.

Tim rubbed his forehead, embarrassed. Jimmy, staring at the brunette's ass, walked through the little mom and pop restaurant, out the front door, to their hiking gear. He lifted his pack and peered back through the door. The cute redhead had brought the change back and was smiling at Tim.

Jimmy rapped his knuckles on the window. When Tim looked up, his face was plastered on the glass with his tongue out.

Tim smiled and sighed, "I'm sorry about him. He's a bit much sometimes."

The waitress stepped closer. When Tim turned, he was eye level with her breasts. Apples, cinnamon, and honey, his favorite scents emanated from her body. Pausing for a brief second to savor his next inhale, he lifted his eyes and met the sparkling sapphires gazing back.

She smiled, "It's okay hun, he ain't the worst we got around here. Are you going to spend another night in town?"

Her face held an unexpected expression of hunger and sweet, but dangerous, longing.

"Naw, I'd better head out and catch up with that shithead friend of mine. He'll never let me hear the end of it if I slept in a soft bed while he 'roughed it' in a tent."

"Well, that's sad, hun. Maybe y'all can stop back through some time?" Her pout was soft and understanding but her eyes were ravenous. Tim's cheeks, and other parts, flushed.

"Thank you for the excellent food and even better service."

Tim stood and stretched, the funk from five days without deodorant assaulting his senses. His arms dropped and a flush of heat rose through his face as the lingering gaze of the cute redhead in the apron vanished into the kitchen. He grabbed the receipt to read the name 'Chloe' printed on the back in purple ink.

The trail alternated between rotten boardwalk and mushy grass. Jimmy had been hiking for an hour when he stopped for a break. The map showed meadow land with small outcroppings of trees but in reality, it was a bit more like a swamp. The air was hot, humid, and still; it stunk like wet earth and sweet decay. No water source appeared marked on the map.

Jimmy sat on a tree trunk along the path. Tall sawgrass bordered stagnant water filled with leaf litter, broken branches, dead trees, cattails, and mosquito larvae. In the dappled sunlight of the afternoon his vision became blurry, dream-like. He dismissed it as the effects of dehydration and haze. He drifted into a daydream about a cute brunette in nothing but an apron when something stirred in the water behind him.

Expecting a frog or large fish to break the surface, he was startled by antlers and hooves. He jumped, grabbed the pistol, and dropped it. The deer spat at him and bounded away through the bog, evaporating in the haze. His heart was racing, pumping adrenaline through his veins into his trembling limbs.

"What the shit Jesus fucking Christ ass was that?" Panting, he reached for his sidearm that lay just short of the water's edge.

He paused as if expecting something to jump from the water.

"There's nothing in that water that can get you. Now, man up." Still shaking, he quickly grabbed and holstered his gun.

He was on edge the rest of the hike. The sun cast long shadows by the time he reached the mouth of the campsite. There was space for two or three tents with a fire pit for cooking in the center.

Exhausted from the wet terrain, he decided to set up camp. There were a couple of flat spots with room to be comfortable, but he chose the smaller one where he could watch the trail for Tim, or anyone else, to come along.

With the tent up, and his pack stowed, Jimmy decided to find water. This time the map showed a spring one hundred feet from the campsite, just before reaching a bog. The spring bubbled out of a small outcropping of rocks and flowed down the path, through brush and sawgrass, into the bog.

Since the incident with the deer, Jimmy kept his gun easily accessible. As he gathered the water, the chipmunks scurrying in the underbrush and the birds and squirrels in the trees were almost deafening. He knew that the animals would go silent if something was on the prowl, but he wasn't taking any chances. Feeling hemmed in by the tall grass near the spring, he reached for his pistol. His nerves calmed when his hand rested on the cool polished chrome of the barrel.

As he walked back to the campsite the hair on his neck became electrified, something watched him. He saw nothing but the spring path and underbrush, his hand drifted to the sidearm once more.

No need to freak. It's just your mind playing tricks and nature doing what nature does, he thought.

Back at camp, he rummaged around the tent for his cooking gear and food. The sound of feet scuffing on the trail broke his culinary pursuit.

"About goddamn time you got-" the remark faded as two hikers entered the campsite.

The redhead reminds me of that waitress with the fun sized knockers, and the brunette must be that other waitress with the delicious can, he thought.

The girls locked on him with cheshire grins and jeweled eyes.

"Sorry, ladies, I thought you were someone else. Water's just down that way about a hundred feet. The spring water is clear but the bog it runs into looks a little sketchy."

They dropped their small packs next to a large tree near the mouth of the campsite, turned to face him and, in unison, said, "Thank you for the tip."

I got a tip for you, ladies.

They crouched and began unpacking their gear, whispering to each other. Dirt and scuffs covered their tent and holes riddled their sleeping bag.

Their stuff is trashed. What the hell happened?

"Hey, uh, not to be nosy or anything but your gear looks banged up. If you want, I'll sleep under the stars, and you can use my tent." Hoping they would take his offer and then offer him a warm place to spend the night. "And, uh, did you guys bring food? If not, I've got plenty to share."

They side-eyed him and smiled.

"Thank you, but we're just fine." The intoxicating southern accent of the brunette stirred something inside him. "We don't need much except company. Can you help us with that?"

Jimmy swallowed hard, not knowing what to say.

"What Sadie means is, would you be willing to stay up with us tonight, hun? Sometimes it takes us a while to fall asleep," the redhead's voice was just as sweet.

"What Chloe is trying to say is, sometimes we get a little scared at night and would love if you'd be able to help us stay safe"

Jimmy was stunned before coming to his senses. "Absolutely," he said, puffing out his chest. "I'd be happy to provide the beautiful Sadie and Chloe safety and warmth tonight."

Both girls raised a seductive eyebrow at his last words, then looked at each other and giggled. Sadie stood, leveled her emerald eyes on Jimmy and asked, "Are you expecting a friend? You greeted us like we were supposed to be someone else." She scanned him from top to bottom, biting her lower lip.

Excitement shot through him. "I'm not sure if he is staying another night in the town a few miles back or not. His ankle was a little sore this morning."

Sadie smiled, "so it's just the three of us then."

She crouched back down to pull a bag of jerky from her pack. Jimmy, a little perplexed about what was happening, began filtering water into his cook pot.

The pot was almost full, but Jimmy wasn't paying attention to it. He noticed, out of the corner of his eye, how the girls fumbled with their tent and sleeping bag.

"Do you ladies need a hand?"

"No thank you, we're getting it. We borrowed this from a friend and didn't have time to practice" Sadie said with a smile and wink.

"It looks like it could fall on you in the night. Are you sure I can't talk you out of using that tent and bag" He asked.

Chloe smiled and shook her head, while Sadie began slowly removing her loose-fitting shirt. He stopped dead. Underneath, she wore a front clasping sports bra and very tight black stretch pants. Grabbing her water bottle, she started walking towards the spring path. The peaks and valleys between her thighs were well defined and, as she walked past, he noticed the bounce to her bra and a hint of pine, amber, and maple syrup, his favorite scents. Her ponytail swished and his pants got a little tighter as he watched her walk towards the spring.

"How long were you waiting before we got here, hun?"

The question startled him so bad that he jumped. Chloe was right behind him, smiling. She too was in black stretch pants but instead of a sports bra she was wearing a string bikini top that was a little too small. He didn't notice when she took off her tee-shirt, or when she crept up behind him. He was too focused on Sadie and her delicious aroma.

Jimmy swallowed hard. "I, uh, maybe an hour." His heart was beating fast, judging by the rapid throbbing in his pants. He needed to get control of himself.

"Oh, that's not too terribly long now, is it?" Chloe asked, twirling a section of her shoulder length red hair around her finger. "I'm glad you weren't by yourself too long. We saw a deer by the trail a ways back. He was a pretty boy, just standing there drinkin', we sat and watched, until something scared him off." Her sparkling blue eyes pinned Jimmy in place. "Did you happen to see any deer when you were coming through the bog?"

"I-- I did. It scared the shit out of me. Almost shot the damn thing with my .45." He moved his hand and touched an empty holster.

What the hell, he thought.

He didn't remember setting the gun down. Panic knifing through his gut.

"That would've been a nice prize."

Another startle, this time from Sadie.

153

"Jesus shit!" Jimmy jumped to the side, grabbing the air in his empty holster. "How the hell are you guys sneaking up on me with the forest so quiet?"

"We're sorry," they said in unison through pouting lips and sad eyes. Taking a step closer to him, Sadie rested a hand on his chest, "We didn't mean to scare you." Her touch was warm, and he inhaled more of her intoxicating odor.

A calm came over him. "Yeah, it's okay," he half smiled, and a black fog darkened his periphery. "We'll all feel safer once we light a fire."

As daylight sank into twilight, the missing pistol was still bugging him. He searched his pack, around his tent, and halfway down the spring path, but it was gone. Resigned to his fate he decided to make dinner. The two girls chewed on the jerky from their pack and Jimmy ate his meal in the glow from the fire pit.

It was getting dark, the forest silent, and all Jimmy could think about was how the three of them would fit in his sleeping bag. As the flames turned to embers, he wondered what Tim would say when he found them the next day.

"Good night, Jimmy." the girls called in unison bringing him back from his thoughts. They stood, their bodies glowing in the dying firelight, and smiled at him before turning their backs, bending over, and ducking into their tent. Jimmy watched the whole performance, pressure building in his pants once more.

"Uh, okay, good night, ladies," was all he could say.

He didn't know how their meager clothing stood up to the chill once the sun set. Imagining them shivering in the night and coming to him for warmth engorged him.

"Goddamn, that would be hot," Jimmy said under his breath. Raspy giggles sounded from the girls and his heart beat faster.

"Well, I'd better hit the hay. It's going to be a long day tomorrow," he announced.

"Good night, Jimmy," came from the girls. He could hear the smile in their teasing and seductive tone.

He tripped walking to his tent, crawled in, and got changed into nothing but a pair of gym shorts. The fire was just a few small logs smoldering and sputtering in the darkness, the forest quiet. He climbed into his sleeping bag and fell asleep to pine, amber, and maple syrup lingering in his thoughts.

The sound of a zipper being opened by deft fingers woke him. He heard a soft giggle and then whispered words, "Come outside, we're waiting for you." His mind exploded with erotic visions as he scrambled out of his sleeping bag.

Jimmy emerged and glimpsed two sets of pale, creamy, ass cheeks disappearing in the night towards the spring.

"This way," they whispered in unison. "Come find us."

The darkness was total. The only sounds he could hear were the trickle of water, the blood pounding in his ears, and giggles that reminded him of fingernails scratching soft wood. As he approached the spring, he saw the backs of both girls moving towards the bog.

"Come find us. Hurry Jimmy, we're waiting."

He quickly continued down the path after them. His foot touched water and he stopped, wondering if he passed them in the dark. Scanning his surroundings yielded nothing but various shapes and shades of black, his night vision not quite enough to pierce the dark.

It was so quiet.

He heard faint raspy giggles. Just visible in the bog were both girls with black liquid up to their chins.

"Can you swim, Jimmy?"

"Like a fish," he answered while stripping off his shorts. He couldn't discern their bodies, but his imagination was conjuring soft skin, warm flesh, and perky full breasts. As a final gesture of the promise of pleasure, Sadie swam closer to the edge. The water, now just grazing the tops of her nipples, caressed her in the rising moonlight.

"Hurry Jimmy," she said. "We're waiting and we're hungry."

Jimmy's mind exploded. His erection dripped while he entered the bog. The water was warm velvet that flowed around as he waded further towards the girls, who were receding into the night.

"Come in deeper Jimmy," came from all directions.

"Where are you?" he asked, water up to his chin.

A smooth hand grasped his cock from around his waist and another, his shoulder. Hard nipples poked and scratched his back and strong legs wrapped around his thighs. He moved his hand to reach whatever part of her body he could when another set of hands, this time from in front, grabbed his wrists.

The girl behind began nibbling and sticking her tongue in Jimmy's ear. He moaned, her lips, soft and silky. A warm rush wormed its way from his ear through his chest, down his core, and through his shaft to the tip. He was floating in nothingness, head swimming in a pool of bliss. The warmth inside, the scent of iron, the soft tug at his ear, and the firm hands were intense but serenely pleasurable.

His eyes eased open. The girl in front stayed just out of view in the darkness. Her silhouette, and the water rippling in front of her, glowed faint, in the dark.

"You wan' sum too?" Jimmy's tongue was thick in his mouth.

"It's okay, hun. She picked you. I'll get the next one."

Chloe's voice, muffled, drifted from far away. As the moon rose higher the shadows began to shrink. Jimmy wanted to view their naked bodies, but his vision was blurred, and his thoughts sluggish. Warm dampness was running down his neck from his ear. The water that lapped at his lower lip tasted like maple syrup and metal.

"Wha.. whas... happen..in?"

Dizzy. So nice.

"Shhh, the forest is sleeping. We don't wanna disturb the critters," Sadie said, right next to his swollen, throbbing, ear.

The haze over Jimmy eased.

The forest, silent.

Chloe let go and he was slowly spun to face Sadie.

Darting forward, one hand reached to find her breast and the other her ass. His mouth lunged for hers.

Both hands sank into muck, the taste of mud and blood enveloped his tongue, and the stench of wet earth and sweet pungent decay lodged in his nose. Jimmy pulled back and opened his stinging eyes.

Staring at him were two milky white eyes, slick green-brown skin, and a twisted bulbous, blistered nose. Black corpse-like lips and sharp needle teeth grinned while a long leech tongue dripped viscous fluid into the water.

"I'm here, Jimmy," Sadie's voice said through putrid lips. "Come get what you deserve."

Before he could scream the teeth and lips closed around his throat and he was pulled beneath the water.

Tim made it to the campsite just before midnight to an inviting fire. Two cute girls were seated in the glow, cooking, but there was no sign of Jimmy.

"Excuse me" said Tim, "did you ladies see another guy, about 6'2", red shirt and cargo pants, pass through? We were supposed to camp here tonight."

The girls, a redhead and brunette that looked a little familiar, shook their heads. "The spring is that way, just before the bog, if you need water," the brunette said as she pointed down a dark path with a kabob stick full of fresh meat.

"It's pretty quiet tonight. You should be able to hear the water trickling."

"Thank you for the tip," Tim said, a bit confused.

The girls softly giggled as he dropped his pack in on the flat spot at the back of the campsite.

He used his flashlight to cut through the dark and started down the spring path. He couldn't see the spring, although there was something shiny like metal in the grass a few yards away. He flicked the light off and listened for the trickling. Following the sound of water, he ended up at the bog.

The moon was up, and he could see the water's edge. His still swollen ankle would feel good in the cool water but then he remembered the bog had leeches. He was about to head towards the campsite when he heard soft footsteps on the path. One of the girls was walking towards him in a bikini top and stretch pants.

"Hey," he said, as she came to a stop next to him. Her red hair shining silver in the moonlight. He caught the slight scent of apples, cinnamon, and honey.

"Hey Tim."

She began untying the strings and removing her bikini top. Her full breasts fell forward as she bent to take off her stretch pants.

"Would you like to go for a dip, hun?"

She righted herself and stood there, waiting for Tim's answer, with the moon highlighting her curves. He scanned her body, pausing at her breasts, stopping at her sparkling blue eyes.

"Is your name Chloe," Tim asked while shedding his hiking clothes.

"It was," she said, letting out a breathy giggle.

Her eyes held him in place as she took his hand and led him into the bog.

Under the Boardwalk
Jayce Maxwell

Sly waved his arm with a flourish and handed the middle-aged white woman her purchase, grinning with all the charm he could muster. "Enjoy those crystals, chère, and be mindful with your spellwork," he drawled in a thick Cajun accent. "Come back to Legba's any time, hear?"

The bell over the door rang as the woman tittered walking out. She was blushing, which was exactly what Sly wanted to see. He knew she had no idea what she was doing with those things, or even what they were, but he didn't care. He'd spread the charm thick and sprinkled in enough bullshit to make the sale. That's the only part he cared about. The women thought they could have him, and they could keep on thinking that as long as they made the register open.

He smoothed out the front of his long, black coat, embossed with silver trim, that cinched in tight over his slender waist. He took off the matching top hat to check his skull makeup.

He was serving Baron Samedi, but sexy.

A bit of down from his top hat's feathers had taken residence on his cheek, back near his ear. How long had that been there? He slipped off one of his velvet black gloves so the white grease paint wouldn't smudge it, picking off the fluff between pristinely manicured nails. The bone white polish matched the makeup on his face, just in case he needed to deglove in front of a customer, and starkly contrasted the deep chestnut of the backs of his hands.

The register sat on a countertop island near the back of the store, with nothing preventing customers from going behind it. Opening the drawer he used for personal items, he slid the mirror and gloves inside, and pulled out a hand rolled cigarette and lighter.

Unlike most stores, the ones that lined the Bayou Waterfront had two entrances. One faced the parking lot and had the main storefront, but the other sat on the back wall, providing easy access to potential customers strolling along the boardwalk. He placed a sign by the register saying he'd be right back, then headed out the rear entrance.

The first tendrils of dusk began to darken the world, and the lampposts kicked on while he smoked. A wooden fence separated the stores from the boardwalk, and someone had laced fairy lights through it. following the fence, the boardwalk was 10 ft wide, very sturdy, and stretched on for a few miles. In between entrances, benches dotted the walk, along with ladders on the opposite side, just in case someone wandered too close to the edge and fell in. the whole thing was designed for tourists, and Sly had to admit that the walkway at night was romantic as fuck.

Only one aspect bothered him. When he stood out on the boardwalk, he was technically over the edge of the Bayou. anything could be living underneath, including gators. Those were the thoughts racing through his head when a scratching beneath his feet made his skin crawl. He darted back past the fence line and turned to survey the spot he'd just vacated.

He saw nothing, but a second bout of scratching, clear as day, made his blood run cold. "Absolutely bloody not," he muttered, his real accent slipping out. Backing away, he continued listening, but he heard nothing else before reaching the door. He wasted no time in making sure the door was locked between him and whatever was out there. No one came to that door after dark anyway. He shivered and pulled down the shade for good measure.

"Do you work here?"

Sly jumped and a small scream escaped his lips. "Yes, sorry," he said, switching back to his light Cajun accent like a second skin. "Something spooked me out there."

"I noticed," said the stranger with a chuckle. Sly scoped him out quickly. The boy was walking sex-on-a-stick. Dark hair, eyes like emeralds, tanned skin, and a smirk on his pretty twink face that promised a great time. The guyliner on his eyes and the leather collar sporting an amethyst on the buckle told Sly just how good a time the boy was willing to have. He looked twenty, maybe, and his well-pressed shirt and pants - all black down to his polished dress shoes - looked like they were tailored to his slender body.

Sly gave him a bow. "My name, handsome, is Sly Fox, and I will give you whatever you want." He wasn't afraid to flirt with this one. With the way he was dressed, he was fishing for a man, or at the very least, fine with a man telling him he looked good.

163

"Jordan," the twink said, "and I just might take you up on that offer, if you look as good without the makeup as you do with it on."

Sly mirrored Jordan's smirk. He liked where this was heading. "First thing's first, chèr, what brings you here today?"

"I need a couple supplies for my altar. Also, does anyone buy that accent?" Jordan set some things on the counter, mostly candles and crystals. His selections had come from the bins his boss had told him were actually used for witchcraft. So the cutie practiced magic.

Sly laughed off the teasing. "Fine," he said, letting his Geordie accent out. No one ever expected him to be British. "You're right. I'm not exactly from this area. Is this everything you need?"

"Apart from your number, yes."

"I'll give you that in the morning, after breakfast," he countered flirt for flirt. He finished up processing Jordan's order and held the bag out to him, not letting go once Jordan's hand was on it. He allowed himself to be pulled closer.

A loud banging against the back entrance made him jump and he couldn't stop the small scream that escaped his mouth. "Why you got this door locked, Sly" called a woman's voice from the other side - one he knew very well. "You know you ain't s'posed to lock up before closin' time."

Sly darted to the door and opened it wide. He could hear Jordan chuckling behind him. "I do apologize, Harri," he apologized to the woman who owned the building, using his fake accent. She was small, but striking in her pinstriped pantsuit.

"Tell me you not gettin' lazy on me, boy," she said, her Creole accent much thicker than his Cajun one, and fully authentic.

"No, Harri. I . . . I heard something out there," he admitted, pointing out back toward the bayou.

She gave him the eye at first, then cracked up at his expense. "You got spooked by the bayou at night. Ain't no one gon' believe you're one of us if you keep caterwaulin' at shadows." She shook her head with a smile. "You got your rent, Sly"

"Yes ma'am," he said, pulling an envelope from his coat's inner pocket. There was no way he would leave it sitting in his personal drawer under the counter. Nothing blocked the customers from that space.

"You're reliable, I'll give you that much." She finally noticed the other person in the store. "You got a customer."

"Harriet, Jordan. Jordan, my landlord and employer, Harriet. Harri for short," Sly said in his most formal Cajun tone. He wasn't allowed to be British for the tourists.

She noticed the bag in his hand. "You here for curiosities, or are you a practitioner?" Sly noticed her accent got far thinner. She was code switching for the potential tourist.

"I'm a witch," he told her simply. "Nice to meet you."

"Likewise. You from around here?"

"A few miles out, but yes," he told her. "My usual place is having stock issues, but you seem to be doing fine here."

Harri turned to Sly, her eyebrow raised. "You used that contact I gave you for supplies?"

"Sure did."

"Good boy." She was clearly pleased he'd brought in stock that other places couldn't.

"My next question is: what scared you out there?"

"I was having a smoke and something started scratching under the boards. I thought it was a gator," Sly admitted.

Harri shook her head. "Ain't no gators for a mile. I keep telling you Auntie Eve laid down a spell to keep them out of the public areas, but you refuse to believe in her power."

"I've heard of Auntie Eve," Jordan chipped in. "If she placed a ward, I guarantee what you heard wasn't a gator." He grinned. "It was probably a Bog Hag."

Harri guffawed. "Oh, I like this boy. You want a job?"

He smirked and looked into Sly's eyes. "I'm sure I'm going to get one later."

Harri paused and glanced between the two men. "I see," she said. "Well, the store closes in an hour. You two head out and get a bite to eat. I'll close up."

"You mean it?" Sly asked.

"Yes, boy! I was young once, and this one's too cute to miss out on. Clean your face and go."

Sly hugged her and darted for the interior stairs that led to his apartment that took up the entire second floor, also rented from Harri. "Keep the outfit!" Jordan yelled after him.

Sly cleaned the makeup off of his face as quickly as he could, grabbed his keys and wallet, and rushed back down.

"Whoa," Jordan said, "you're even hotter without the makeup." Sly felt the heat rise to his face, grateful his dark skin hid the blush. What he couldn't hide was the smile threatening to split his face in two.

Sly took them out the front entrance and they walked the well lit commercial sidewalk, a line of buildings between them and the bayou. They kept the conversation light for the few blocks it took to reach the outdoor cafe. At night, the place was hard to miss with its hanging lanterns, twinkling lights, zydeco music playing over the speakers, and the soft din of patrons having a good time.

The hostess asked if they wanted to sit near the water. Sly shook his head, but Jordan laughed. "Yes, we'd like to sit by the water," he told her, taking Sly's hand. "I promise you, there's nothing that'll hurt you while I'm here." Sly allowed himself to be led to the table. Being so close to the dark water made his heart race, but so did the hand Jordan placed on his thigh after they sat. The fear melted away, replaced by lower emotions, and he relaxed.

"So, Jordan," Sly asked. "What in God's name is a Bog Hag?"

Their waitress set their drinks down and he took a sip before answering. "Some legends say they're little more than predators, grabbing anyone they can reach and pulling them underwater, killing their prey with poisoned claws and drowning. Some legends, though, are more interesting. They paint Bog Hags as more genie-like, granting wishes in exchange for favors or gifts."

"So they're good women?"

"Women?" Jordan asked.

"Well, you said they were hags."

Jordan pursed his lips. "Tradition only uses hags and witches to refer to females in order to shame women into being subservient. They make men feel superior to the "scary" women."

Sly held up his hands. "Sorry. Didn't mean to offend.

Jordan sat back in his chair and took a breath. "It's fine. It's not your fault the patriarchy has taught you women are evil and men are just. Do me a favor, though, and try to unlearn it."

"I can do that."

Jordan leaned forward and took Sly's hand. He kissed the back of it and grinned. "If you had one wish, something purely for personal gain, not lame like world peace, what would it be?"

The conversation pivot was odd to Sly, but he'd play along. Jordan probably didn't want to talk about the gender divide anymore. Sly gave the question a moment to breathe. "Harri said I could buy the store from her if I did well enough with it. I've never had a home of my own, let alone a business. I think I'd wish for that: for a successful business."

"What would you be willing to sacrifice for it, if you were making a trade with a Bog Hag?"

"Sacrifice? I don't have anything worthwhile. What would a Bog Hag want from me anyway?"

"Your first born?" Jordan asked.

"Unless you can get pregnant, that's never going to be a thing. What happens if I never sleep with a woman?"

"Probably nothing good," Jordan admitted. "How about something obscure, like your dying breath?"

Sly raised an eyebrow. "Wouldn't that mean they'd just kill me on the spot?"

"Not necessarily. What if they promised not to kill you for it?"

Sly pondered the hypothetical offer. In the scenario, he could live out his life, and his debt wouldn't be due until his final day. "Alright, I'd give my dying breath for the success of my store," he finally said.

The lantern hanging over their table flashed as the bulb inside popped, and Sly could swear the amethyst on Jordan's collar glowed violet for a moment. Several people shouted as their table became the center of attention, but the commotion died down quickly once everyone realized it was just a power surge.

"Maybe we should stop playing this game," Jordan said under his breath. "I think something might have been trying to take us seriously."

It was Sly's turn to laugh. "Now who's spooked at nothing?"

Jordan replied by sticking his tongue out and taking the last spoonful of his soup. Sly barely remembered the meal, he'd been having such a good time. He paid the bill and the two of them left the restaurant.

"Can we take the boardwalk back? The lights are so pretty." Jordan's voice was soft and irresistible, and Sly was far more emboldened than he had been earlier. He steered them toward the water in response, and Jordan leaned his head on Sly's shoulder as they strolled.

They were barely out of the ambience of the restaurant when Sly heard the scratching again. He tensed. "That's the sound Do you hear it?

Jordan took a step to the side and gave Sly a "you're not serious" look. "That could be literally anything," he said. "It's probably a rat or something."

An unholy croaking sound followed, longer than any toad he'd ever heard, and hollow as a dead log. "There you go," Jordan told him. "That's just a bayou frog. It's probably trying to lay some eggs down there. Must be mating season."

Sly could still feel his hand's shaking, despite Jordan's explanation and demeanor. Jordan took his hands and pulled him in close, briefly touching their lips together. "Snap out of it, Sexy, or you'll miss your own mating season." Sly exhaled as fingers traced the hardening lump in his pants.

"I'm back," he said.

"Good," Jordan said, his sexual leer deepend as he stepped back and pulled Sly farther down the boardwalk.

"You know," Jordan said after a minute or two, "I don't know your real name. I doubt it's Sly Fox."

"It kind of is. Sly is a shortened form of the name Sylvester. My last name is Fawkes, like Guy Fawkes."

"Heh," Jordan mused. "That's actually quite clever, and so very, very British, Sylvester Fawkes."

"Just . . . don't try the accent, okay?" Sly pleaded jokingly.

"Oh, so you're the only one allowed to have a horrible fake accent?" The teasing was gentle, but Sly brought his hand to his chest and feigned being scandalized. "Seriously, though, you're not Creole or Cajun, but you dress like Baron Samedi, you don't believe in magic, and you're scared of the bayou. Why did Harri hire you? Not being rude, just curious. Aren't you afraid of appropriation?"

"I'm here for the tourists," Sly admitted. "Besides, I think I play my role brilliantly. Harri picked an actor who could put on a show in the fake store so the tourists would stay out of the real places - the places that aren't for the casuals and non-believers. I wave my hands and give them my best Fred Astaire moves, and I dazzle them into thinking they've experienced true Creole culture, and they leave the locals alone."

"Makes sense," Jordan said. Their pace was back to a casual stroll now that Jordan had calmed him down. "So why have real supplies mixed into your stock?"

"So practitioners like you can still resupply if needed. Not everything needs to be faked."

"But you don't believe in any of it," Jordan said softly.

171

"I don't need to," Sly said. "I'm just the window dressing." He could make out his building from where they were. The store lights were off, but an exterior stairway led to a landing on the second floor, where a welcoming light beckoned. Bless Harri for leaving that on for him.

A splash in the swamp just past the lip of the boardwalk made Sly jump. He sped up, trying to pull Jordan with him. "Sly," he said, but Sly didn't respond. "Sly!" This time his arm was jerked back, stopping his momentum. "Chill out. It was just another frog." Sly turned to face his date, who had stopped walking altogether. "Why are you trying to make a life in a place you're afraid of?" Jordan asked. "There's nothing out here but us and small animals."

Sly froze. About ten feet behind Jordan, a black, slimy arm reached out of the water by the emergency ladder. It gripped the railing and pulled, making the other arm and a head emerge. Once the mouth was clear, it let forth the same chilling, gargling croak he'd heard near the restaurant, but this time it was much louder.

"Jordan, come over here fast," he ordered. "It's very much not a frog." Jordan whipped his head back, saw what was coming out of the bayou, and ran to Sly. The body, shaped like a human, but slick with black muck, slapped its first foot onto the boardwalk. As it did, the murky gunk sloughed off, revealing raw muscle beneath. Skinless.

He grabbed Jordan's hand and they both sprinted for Sly's home. Sly jammed his hand into the pocket of his coat, gripping his keys for dear life. There would be no losing or dropping them in this chase. Reaching the top, Sly focused on flipping to the correct key and getting the door open. Shoving Jordan through, he darted in and locked it behind them. Only then did he take a moment to look back. The lumbering creature hadn't even shambled halfway to them. Good. He closed the curtains and turned the light off.

"What the hell was that?" he asked. "That sure as hell wasn't a frog."

"Don't know and don't want to know," Jordan said. "Is there any other way for it to get inside?"

"I'll go downstairs and make sure everything's locked up." The inside landing had three doors. One led to the outside landing, where the just were, one led to his apartment, and the third led to the inside stairs, which would take him into the store. Jordan waited at the landing.

Sly darted through the store, checking the two entrances and every window, making sure they were closed and locked. For good measure, he pulled down all the blinds, but cutting off the illumination from the parking lot and boardwalk made navigating the store harder. He was glad he knew it so well, and he only knocked one thing over trying to make it back to the stairs. He'd pick it up in the morning if they lived.

"Are you still there?" Jordan called down after him.

"Yeah, almost done." With the last window checked, he returned to Jordan, letting both of them into his apartment. He locked that door as well for good measure.

They stood by the door, in the dark, with Sly trying to catch his breath. Sly reached for the light switch, but Jordan stopped him with a gentle hand. He shook his head and put a finger to his lips, which was clearly visible due to the ambient orange glow from outside. "Lights and noise bring attention, "Jordan whispered. "Is this door the only way in on this floor?"

"Yeah. My bedroom has a trunk with a fire ladder if there's an emergency. There's no fire escape otherwise."

"That's not up to code."

Sly snorted involuntarily. He wasn't sure if Jordan had meant it as a joke, but it was too out of place not to be funny. Jordan snickered as well, but cut it short. He motioned for them to move away from the door. The living area was just past the entryway, and a sofa faced the door. They waited, listening intently for the creature, until they could hear it shuffling outside the second door.

Croak!

Both of them jumped, and Jordan gripped Sly's forearm. It sounded like it was right in front of them, it was so loud. Sly could feel Jordan's black lacquered nails digging in for dear life. The twink nuzzled in close for safety.

SLAM!

They both screamed as the creature pounded against the door. Jordan jumped over the back of the sofa, leaving burning tracks where his nails had been. He'd drawn blood, but Sly could forgive him for that.

Sly tried to join Jordan behind the sofa, but he couldn't make himself get up. Some lack of impulse, of urgency, glued him to the seat. The sounds around him: Jordan's whimpering, the banging on the door, the croaks from the creature, all lengthened and dropped lower in pitch.

"Is it warping sound?" Sly asked, his tongue heavy and thick, mashing the words inside his mouth.

Jordan stopped making noise and stood, walking calmly around the sofa, to face Sly and turn his back to the door. Was he smiling? Straddling Sly's lap, Jordan slowly unbuttoned Sly's coat and shirt, sliding them down his shoulders. What the hell was he doing? Jordan slid his fingers down Sly's torso and unbuckled his belt, finishing the job by opening his pants. Showing more strength than Sly would have ever expected from the skinny twink, he lifted Sly to pull his clothes away.

Once Sly was naked, Jordan slipped out the door. The lock clicked on the exterior door, which Jordan held open for the beast. He returned to the room, the monster trailing him like a puppy.

"What is it? Who are you?" Sly rasped, barely able to push the words out.

"Save your breath, Sylvester. You have so few of them left," Jordan warned. "Since you clearly haven't figured it out, I'd like you to meet Jordan - the real one. Doesn't his skin look lovely on me?" Whoever this person was, he stripped out of his clothing with little haste. The last thing he removed was the leather collar with the violet gem. Sly's breath tightened, his breaths coming slow and shallow.

The stranger who'd been posing as Jordan turned his back to Sly, revealing a seam that started under his hairline and disappeared in the crack of his rear. He tugged at it and slid the hood from his head. The texture of the skin he revealed reminded Sly of the sticks and branches that got pulled out of the swampy mire below the surface of the bayou. Black with rot and dripping with muck, he knew it would also be as hard as wood. With gentle care, he let it slip to the floor like an empty shirt.

Reaching down, he handed the skin back to Jordan. "Put your skin on before it dries out," he ordered, putting the leather collar back on. Jordan started to obey, croaking frequently, as the impostor turned back to face Sly.

Sly's bowels emptied.

It was covered head to toe in the rotten bark, but the limbs were far more spindly than humanly possible, yet Sly knew how strong they were already. The emerald green eyes, which had looked so pretty coming from Jordan's face, now swam with a nauseating glow the color of dying grass. Its nose was missing, mere slits in its place, but below that, a mouth hung wide from ear to ear. Ropy tendrils barely kept the lower jaw from falling off of its head, and hundreds of piranha-like teeth lined both the top and bottom.

"You," it told Sly, impossibly forming words with a mouth unsuited for the task. It climbed back up onto him, straddling him as before, but this time, the nauseating slime pressed into his thighs and rested on his manhood. Their faces were inches apart.

"Ask me why I know so much about bog hags." It started to cackle maniacally.

"You lied," Sly managed to croak out.

"No, Sylvester. You just weren't listening to the truth. Besides, I think I played my role brilliantly." The hag used Sly's voice to mock him with his own words. It leaned in closer and inhaled, extracting the scant air remaining in Sly's lungs. He tried to take a breath, but could only croak. He was going to die. He'd promised his dying breath to this thing as a game, and now it was going to suffocate him. The pain from being

176

unable to breathe racked his entire chest. Terror filled him, knowing he was surrounded by precious, life giving air, but couldn't take any to save himself.

Jordan, now reskinned, stepped into view to the bog hag's side, stark naked, and still very cute. His eyes, the real ones, brown and filled with panic, bulged as he tried to take in breaths. Was that what Sly looked like now?

"As I said," the hag explained, "I didn't lie. I'm not killing you at all. You're suffocating, yes, but I have your dying breath, which keeps you tethered to the living realm. Like pretty little Jordan there, you're trapped in your final moment, doomed to reach for a breath that will never reach you, for eternity. You. Can't. Die." With each of those last words, it booped him on the nose with a slimy wooden finger.

"You see, I need your skins to pass as human, but they're just so ephemeral without their bodies to keep them vital. Without you, they'll rot away in days. You see, I need you alive. No lies were told. As for the precious shop you sold yourself to me over: I'll continue to run it. It will have the financial success you paid for. So many tourists coming through, hoping some magic or another will solve their problems. So many wishes for me to exploit."

The bog hag lifted him effortlessly, laying him out face down on the sofa. "Now it's time for me to get dressed."

Sly tried to scream as a searing hot talon dug a line down the center of his back. CROAK!

CHERRY RED
NICOLE FORD THOMAS

The dock and the house trailer were in a race to see which would rot into the swamp faster, and Johnny was counting on the trailer going first. Despite the creaks and protests of the decaying wood, Johnny slouched back in his fishing chair, a frayed, nylon relic from the 80's. August on the bayou wasn't fit for man nor beast, but evenings on the bayou were left to something worse than both.

After the first dozen cans of Budweiser, Johnny hardly noticed the mosquitos and those damned flies. No amount of alcohol could mask the Louisiana humidity, though, making his bare chest glisten with dirt and sweat.

From deep inside the pocket of his cargo shorts, a series of buzzes nudged him out of the heat stupor. "J, the police are looking for you," the text read. "Shelby's still missing. They know you left the bar together."

He sucked his teeth before sliding the phone back into his pocket. He knew no one in this town could keep their goddamn mouths shut. The remaining beer slid down his throat, hot and foamy. Lean muscles rippled along his arms as he lofted the empty can, before the dead air brought it down a few feet away to bounce off Shelby's forehead.

The flies stirred, allowing her milky eyes to stare up at him.

Johnny pulled the last can of beer from the cardboard box. As he popped the tab open, a small snake slithered across Shelby's twisted, purple neck. His drunken gaze returned to the bayou while he waited.

Shelby looked older than seventeen in the neon lights of the bar. Her blond ringlets bounced around her jaw when she laughed, those cherry red lips glossed like glass, caressing the clear, plastic shot glasses. But it was the the combination of the white shirt with embroidered cherries she had tied so tightly below her breasts and the cut-off denim shorts, tight enough to be second skin and short enough to let the globes of her ass cheeks play peek-a-boo from the bottom, that stoked his desire.

No one wondered why a minor was there or moved to tell her to leave. It left Johnny feeling protective of her, wanting to take her somewhere safe. They danced all night, Johnny slipping her shots of Fireball when no one was looking, and when she placed those cherry red nails on his chest and whispered in his ear, "Let's get out of here," he knew he found an angel on Earth.

An hour later, as Johnny pulled at the button holding those tiny shorts to her body, his night took a turn. Shelby clammed up, muttering bullshit about going too fast, and how she'd better get home because her grandma was gonna notice she wasn't in her room at sunrise.

"It won't take long," he told her, "then I'll drive you back." But it wasn't enough for Shelby. She wouldn't trust Johnny to take good care of her. His cherry angel, his Shelby. That's when the screaming started.

Johnny couldn't tolerate the sound of a woman screaming. It was a sound he heard as he fell asleep at night, since Becca, the brunette. And Jessica, the raven-haired beauty before that. When the need to silence the screaming overtook his need to release the pressure in his pants, Johnny wrapped one hand around Shelby's mouth and nose, and another squeezed her throat.

"Shelby, hush," he hissed, "I got you. You're my girl now."

She brought a knee up to connect with his balls, and when he rolled off in pain, Shelby bolted from the trailer into the first morning light. She scrambled to get into his car and lock the doors behind her, but Johnny was quicker and pulled her from the front seat by those pretty gold curls. Her screams filled his head as he dragged her to the bank of the bayou. After pulling a baseball bat from its hiding place in the car, Johnny brought it down on Shelby's neck, again and again.

Finally, the screaming stopped.

The bulge in Johnny's pants throbbed harder, but he wasn't a sicko. Once Shelby stopped moving, her body was good for nothing but feeding gators.

He drank greedily from the beer can and waited for the gators or the police, but Johnny never expected the wait to stretch longer than his beer. He drained the last of the final can and stared into the stagnant water.

The footsteps on the dock startled him from his drunken haze. When a delicate hand with cherry red nails lowered an icy beer in front of his face, he took it and huffed. He knew those nails from the way they scratched at his face and arms earlier that morning.

Shelby moved between Johnny and the water, where he could finally take in her beauty one last time. Her blond curly hair bobbed along her jawline and the thick lips glossed cherry red smiled at him sweetly. Even the denim cut-off shorts were buttoned back around her hips, and the white shirt with its embroidered cherries was tied back between her breasts. His cherry angel.

"I got you another one, sugar," she said, sweetly.

Johnny grunted. "That's mighty kind of you, Shelby. I was getting thirsty." He cracked open the top and guzzled the first half of the can before noticing a thick, salty taste.

Shelby's delicate hand tipped the can back up against his mouth. "You gotta drink it all, shug."

The dregs of the can tasted like dirty swamp water and spit, but Johnny did as Shelby said and was rewarded with a feeling of tranquility settling over his mind and body. Let the gators come. Let the police come. He was just fine now that Shelby was there.

"Yes," Shelby said. "You'll be just fine." She tossed the empty can with the others.

A dark haze settled over the periphery of Johnny's vision, but he still noticed something odd about the girl. Every step of her bare feet left watery footprints and mud on the dock. "Shelby, how come your feet are wet?" The buzzing in his pocket nudged him angrily.

"You'd better check that, Johnny."

The small screen lit up his face in the fading light, announcing another text. "If I find out you had anything to do with that girl's disappearance, I swear–" Johnny stopped reading and threw his phone into the water.

"They're coming for me, Shelby," he said.

"Who is, darlin'?" Her creamy thighs spread across his lap as she straddled his legs.

Johnny wrapped his dirty hands around her hips, pulling her closer. "The police, I reckon."

"Well, what could they want with you?" Those cherry red nails he loved twisted hanks of his hair around, before scratching gently against his head.

Johnny fought the dark vignette cloaking his vision. "I killed you, Shelby, sure as shit. I killed you because you wouldn't stop screaming. If you would have just let me take care of you right, this never would have happened."

"That's true," Shelby said, those red lips spreading into a wicked grin, "but I'm not dead, Johnny. I'm right here with you." Her hands slid down his sweaty chest, coming to rest on his growing erection. "But if you need somewhere to hide, I'll hide you. Deep, deep inside of me."

"I might need to lay low for a while," he said. The dark vignette crowded Johnny's sight, but the euphoria returned as blood moved from one head to another. "You know a place I can go?"

"Sure," Shelby said before nibbling his neck. "You can come stay with me as long as you like. It'll just be me, you, and my sisters. Don't you want to meet my sisters, Johnny?"

"Tell you the truth, I didn't know you had sisters. But I bet you're the prettiest one." An ephemeral thought nagged Johnny's mind, unable to break through the haze. A voice whispered *danger*, but all he saw through the dark haze was his cherry red angel, finally ready to give him what she promised by putting on those damn shorts in the first place.

Shelby laughed as she teased her way down from Johnny's lap, kissing and licking salt from his chest, while her nimble hands worked open the front of his cargo shorts.

The hot, dank air of the swamp felt cool on his cock as Shelby pulled it free. When that pouty, glossed mouth wrapped around his skin, his head lolled back at the sensation. The girl was experienced, despite her age. She knew just where to lick and nibble to drive a man wild.

When the hot liquid rolled down his thighs, he blinked away the haze. He couldn't remember finishing, but when every move Shelby made was bliss, who could blame him?

His eyes struggled to focus as Shelby pulled away, holding in her hand a bloody lump of flesh he recognized as his own penis. Pleasure rolled through him.

"Do you want more?" she asked as Johnny's blood ran down her chin.

Everything was fine.

Danger.

Everything was fine.

"Yes," he said as he watched her raise his cock to her lips and lick the blood dripping from the tip. "Shelby, what was in that beer?"

Shelby threw the amputated penis onto the freshly skinned corpse behind them, right where he left her. Only she still had her skin when the flies came.

Danger.

"Gators got her after all," he said, looking at the cherry red of muscles. "Probably fried her skin up and made cracklins."

Police sirens cut through the noise of the nighttime bayou. Johnny startled in his chair, but Shelby deftly soothed his fears.

"Nothing to worry about, sugar," she said. "I'm just fine, right here in front of you."

"Baby, it's time to go," Johnny said.

Danger.

"You want to run away with me?" Shelby coaxed. "You want to follow me where no one will ever find you?"

Too late, Johnny. She found you first.

"Yes," he answered. The dark haze blocked all but a pinprick of his vision, but he could see the red and blue flashing lights approaching. "I'll follow you, Shelby, but where are we going?"

185

"Just right here in the water, shug. Me and my sisters live on the other side of the water." Shelby licked the blood from her hand as she pulled Johnny up from his chair. He clutched his pants to keep them from falling off, and noticed his lap was covered in blood, too.

She found you. The hag found you first.

"The water'll wash that away," he said as Shelby took his hand, leading into the bayou.

"Water washes everything away, Johnny."

They waded in the black muck up to his waist before Shelby let go of Johnny's hand. Her curls swirled as her head dipped below the water. Deeper and deeper she went.

Danger. Too late, Johnny.

A hollow version of Shelby floated to the surface. Her skin filled with water and twisted in the current. An empty shell, discarded. His cherry red angel.

When Shelby rose again, her body was slick like a leach, and iridescent black like an oil spill. Her hair was no longer blond ringlets, but instead deep green streaks, like the plants that grew on the muddy bottom of the bog and tangled his feet. Her webbed fingers reached for him, cutting four splices across his chest, causing blood to run freely into the water. Her cherry red eyes stared at him hungrily.

Johnny fell backward in the water, splashing around to get back on his feet.

Danger.

"It's still me, sugar," the hag said in Shelby's voice. "We're almost there."

She pulled him close to her slimy body, and the putrid stench of wet decay filled his nostrils. Her tongue lapped inside of his mouth, causing euphoria to course through his veins once again.

Everything was fine.

"Are you ready?" the hag asked in Shelby's sweet voice.

"I don't–" Johnny said as the swamp witch opened her black mouth wide, showing rows of pointed teeth circling down her throat. *Danger.* He writhed pathetically in her grip as her teeth descended on his face, biting away a chunk of his cheek. He felt the blood running down his neck and chest, but only bliss remained. "Yes," Johnny said. "I'm ready."

Webbed hands shot out of the water, digging nails into his skin like hooks before pulling him under the water. The ripples on the surface of the dark water sparkled red and blue, but Johnny was gone. Everything was fine.

ABOUT THE AUTHORS

Devon Gambrell

Thank you for reading this short horror. Devon Gambrell usually writes dark fantasy and steampunk with snarky female leads and a splash of romance. She is also the founder of All Call Indie: a database of freelancers for indie authors and one-third chair of the Authortube Writing Conference. She can be found on Instagram and Ream Stories, or sign up for her monthly Snippets & Spoilers newsletter.

www.dgambrell.com/links
www.substack.com/allcallindie
www.authortubewritingconference.com

Karla Hailer

Karla Hailer writes steampunk, paranormal romance, and all kinds of fiction and non-fiction under her name and pen names. She lives outside of Boston with her husband, her cat, Mr. Odins and the spirit of her furry purry roly poly ball of love kitty, Mr. Data. She is a recovering journalist and former fifth grade teacher. You can find her steampunk fiction on Substack and Ream Stories and can find more at https://cogsignition.com/francesdelisle/ or https://linktr.ee/francesdelisle?utm_source=linktree_admin_share Come listen to her weekly short story podcast Aether Tales by Frances DeLisle on most podcast platforms.

C.L Hart

C. L. Hart is an editor who writes or a writer who edits. She lives in a small rural town in northeastern Colorado in a building that has been a hotel, a house of ill repute, a hospital, a boarding house for teachers, and a bed and breakfast. She writes Lovecraftian fantasy, dystopian sci-fi, horror, and speculative fiction with the occasional sweet romance thrown in to upset the cosmic apple cart. When not rehabilitating eldritch horrors, Ms. Hart enjoys being crafty and making baked goods that she hopes will be palatable to someone besides the eldritch horrors. Find C. L. Hart at naughtynetherworldpress.start.page

S.D. Huston

S.D. Huston is a fantasy romance and fantasy author with a passion for writing about broken characters who face adversity to become a better version of themselves. And there may or may not be Dragons, but there's always love to find ;) Follow her for free on Ream, and get access to novellas set in this same world: https://reamstories.com/sdhuston
Follow S.D. Huston's new Kickstarter even if you can't buy anything later, following helps with the algorithm!
https://www.kickstarter.com/projects/sdhuston/a-curse-of-wings-and-gems/
All S.D. Huston's links: https://linktr.ee/sdhuston

Katy Manz

Katy Manz has always dreamed of being a romance writer. She wants to bring the stories created in
her mind to a world of readers who would fall in love with her characters as much as she has. Did you enjoy Beware The Bog Hag? These characters appear in the Choice Verses Fate series, which is available on Amazon and Audible. Keep
looking for more books in this series and future series to come.
Sign up for her newsletter at https://BookHip.com/SANLGMH
Follow Katy Manz on Amazon at www.amazon.com/author/katymanz
Find her at https://linktr.ee/katymanz

Jayce Maxwell

Jayce Maxwell is a ginger hermit who went into hiding after collecting enough souls and turning them into freckles.
Now the souls play out the stories in his head.
His anthology submission was sent to the un-editor via a series of carrier ravens on dark and stormy nights.

J. Noble

J. Noble is a Multi-Genre Author living in Alabama. She loves to spend her time going on adventures with her partner and exploring the beautiful forests and lake areas she lives near. When she isn't exploring, she is writing and working on the several book ideas that she has in her head.

https://linktr.ee/J.Noble

Jenna O'Malley

Jenna O'Malley, your Soul Writer, blends sci-fi/fantasy with dashes of romance and nerdy references to create raw stories about diverse characters throughout time and space. The worlds she weaves highlight issues including women's rights, the importance of all voices in leadership, LGBTQIA+ alliance, mental health awareness, and anti-racism.

Her first pentalogy, The Merna Annals, addresses a few societal norms through the eyes of five immortal species forced to work together to avoid extinction. The question that started it all?

What happened to magic and all of its creatures--paranormal, mythical, celestial, or otherwise--according to human history? This series is fit for fans of tabletop RPGs such as Dungeons and Dragons, Pathfinder, and Vampire: The Masquerade

or for fans of J. R. Ward, George R. R. Martin, and J. R. R. Tolkien. She also helps fellow creatives to (re)set their processes and businesses to doing what they love most in soul bard mode through her modalities as a trauma-informed educator, editor, content creation nerd, and book/bookish business coach.

https://www.jennathesoulwriter.com

Kay Parquet

Meet Kay Parquet, a Southern storyteller with a passion for adventure and a passport full of stamps. Growing up in a military family, she experienced life across the globe, and these adventures fuel her imaginative writing. Kay loves blending fantasy with the future, inspired by her early love for comic books, cartoons, and Star Trek fan fiction. When she's not writing, she's a gamer with a soft spot for dogs, convinced they're the secret rulers of the world.

www.kayparquet.com

https://museink.substack.com/

Rita Slanina

Rita Slanina is the author of the Harbor Excursions novella series, https://bit.ly/48AM2en &, an Amazon bestseller in its category, upon its debut, The Music & Lyrics: How-To Guide To Songwriting. https://bit.ly/45NWPlm

Rita is also a commercial actress & currently co-starring in the theatrical play, Don't Drink the Water by Woody Allen.

https://patagoniacreativearts.org/tin-shed-theater/

Rita Slanina is also active in the #authortube space offering up lifestyle content and sometimes wears weird socks.

Find out more on the blog: www.ritaslanina.com

E.L. Summers

E.L. Summers is native to Baltimore, Maryland and has been writing for over twenty years. She is a blind author and writes poetry, paranormal romance, and urban fantasy. Her debut novel, HUNTED: The Immortal's Kiss, was cowritten with Luna Nyx Frost and is available on Amazon.

E.L Summers inspires creativity and imagination in others with her writing by providing lush details for all senses. Her inspiration comes from nature, fantasy, paranormal literature, and a diverse music collection ranging from pop, showtunes, and punk rock. She also loves reading about fantasy, magic, mythology, faeries, mermaids, and dragons.

E.L Summers published a fantasy anthology titled Realm of Enchantments: A Mystic Anthology and a collection of poetry titled Ignited Melodies: A Book of Poetry. She has had several poems featured in Maryland's Best Emerging Poets 2019 by Z Publishing and Fae Thee Well: An Anthology and Rogues and Rebels: An Anthology both published by Dreampunk Press.

Kyle Thomas

Kyle is new to writing, but not to storytelling. His stories stem from his experience in life as an Eagle Scout, husband, father, and U.S. Marine. He will have more to say when he retires from his day job. Until then, readers will have to glean what they can from his writing.

http://instagram.com/drknight513

Nicole Ford Thomas

Nicole Ford Thomas spends a large portion of her day communing with the voices in her head. Occasionally, she takes the time to write down what they say. When she's not writing, she's likely off somewhere, screaming into the void. She lives in Northeast Ohio with her husband, lots of pets, and a ghost named Roger.

http://youtube.com/c/nicolefordthomas

Cass Voit

Cass Voit wears a lot of hats, but for now, we'll talk about her writing. Based in the Northern Virginia area, she is a self published horror author three times over, but two more chilling stories are coming down the chute. Titles she has worked on include Cyberpunk Supernatural Thriller "HOP35CH35T", Urban Fantasy Thriller "Flambeau", and Psychological Horror Novela "Shadow of the Fae." In her free time, she formats books for other independent authors while sitting on the couch with her orange cats and her Graphic Design Professor Husband watching funny things. However, when she is alone, she will break out the horror movies. She can be contacted on most social media as her pen name Sako Tumi.

M.M. Ward

M.M. Ward, an indie author who started writing as part of her stroke recovery because she lost most of her ability to use language. She writes in a variety of genres while living on her small farm on the Colorado prairie.

193

Amazon page https://www.amazon.com/M.M.-Ward/e/B07NTYTVP2

Ko-fi page https://ko-fi.com/penumbramine/

Twitter https://twitter.com/PenumbraMine/

Facebook Page Author M.M. Ward

https://www.facebook.com/authormmward/

Sam Wicker

Sam is an author of romantic fantasy, but sometimes dabbles in other genres such as sci-fi, horror, and mystery. Growing up in the mountains of North Carolina, she's studied and worked in several things; broadening her knowledge of the world and people in order to twist them up and plop them down in another form in her works. She lives with her loving and supportive husband nicknamed Gonzo (not from the Muppets), and her adopted furbaby Kona in the foothills of North Carolina. Writing, reading, gaming, crocheting, and learning new things are her hobbies and life. Find out more about her, her works, and more through the links in her linktree here: https://linktr.ee/writersamwicker
Read her works and support her on
Ream: https://reamstories.com/samwicker
To keep up with her doings and goings subscribe to her YouTube here: https://www.youtube.com/c/WriterSamWicker